"You, Taylor Carmic[...] [...] walking wrong." Hi[...] [...] mouth. "So tell me what else is on y[...] of banned substances."

"Men like you."

"Is that right?" His eyes on hers, he lowered the champagne bottle back into the fountain. Somehow, without her even noticing how he'd done it, he'd moved closer to her. His dark head was between her and the sun and all she could see were those wicked eyes tempting her toward the dark side.

"What are you doing?"

"Testing a theory." His mouth moved closer to hers and suddenly she struggled to breathe.

"What theory?"

"I want to know whether two wrongs make a right." His smile was the last thing she saw before he kissed her.

SICILY'S CORRETTI DYNASTY

The more powerful the family...the darker the secrets!

Harlequin Presents® introduces the Correttis: Sicily's
most scandalous family!

The Empire

Young, rich and notoriously handsome, the Correttis' legendary
exploits regularly feature in Sicily's tabloid pages!

The Scandal

But how long can their reputations withstand the glaring heat of the
spotlight before their family's secrets are exposed?

The Legacy

Once nearly destroyed by the secrets cloaking their thirst for power,
the new generation of Correttis are riding high again—and no
disgrace or scandal will stand in their way...

Sicily's Corretti Dynasty

Collect all eight volumes!

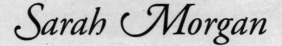

Sarah Morgan

AN INVITATION TO SIN

SICILY'S
CORRETTI
DYNASTY

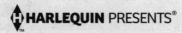

HARLEQUIN PRESENTS®

Recycling programs
for this product may
not exist in your area.

ISBN-13: 978-0-373-13152-5

AN INVITATION TO SIN

Copyright © 2013 by Harlequin Books S.A.

Special thanks and acknowledgment are given to Sarah Morgan
for her contribution to Sicily's Corretti Dynasty series.

Printed in U.S.A.

All about the author...
Sarah Morgan

USA TODAY bestselling author **SARAH MORGAN** writes lively, sexy stories for both Harlequin Presents® and Medical Romance.

As a child Sarah dreamed of being a writer, and although she took a few interesting detours on the way, she is now living that dream. With her writing career she has successfully combined business with pleasure and she firmly believes that reading romance is one of the most satisfying and fat-free escapist pleasures available. Her stories are unashamedly optimistic and she is always pleased when she receives letters from readers saying that her books have helped them through hard times.

RT Book Reviews has described her writing as "action-packed and sexy" and has nominated her books for their Reviewers' Choice Awards and their "Top Pick" slot.

Sarah lives near London with her husband and two children, who innocently provide an endless supply of authentic dialogue. When she isn't writing or reading Sarah enjoys music, movies and any activity that takes her outdoors.

Readers can find out more about Sarah and her books from her website, www.sarahmorgan.com. She can also be found on Facebook and Twitter.

Other titles by Sarah Morgan available in ebook:

Harlequin Presents®

DEFYING THE PRINCE *(The Santina Crown)*
A NIGHT OF NO RETURN
  (The Private Lives of Public Playboys)
WOMAN IN A SHEIKH'S WORLD
  (The Private Lives of Public Playboys)
SOLD TO THE ENEMY

For my editor Lucy Gilmour, with thanks.
Of all the things we shared over the years,
winning the RITA was the best. xx

CHAPTER ONE

'ZACH? WHERE THE hell are you? You'd better not bail on me because I don't think I can do this without you. Any moment now I'm going to give in and eat carbs and that is going to be the end of this dress. When you get this message, call me.' The phone almost slipped from her sweaty palm and Taylor gripped it tightly. It was just a wedding. Just a bunch of people she didn't care about and who certainly didn't care about her. It shouldn't be enough to put her in this much of a state. She was only here because the producer of her latest film had insisted on it.

She tried to take a deep breath but the dress wouldn't allow her chest to expand. The designer had sewn her into it and then told her to send a text when she needed a bathroom break.

The Sicilian heat scalded her bare back and Taylor rolled her eyes at the absurdity of the situation. It was too hot to be sewn into anything and she'd kill before she allowed someone in the bathroom with her, which basically meant she couldn't eat or drink. Not that she ate much anyway. The discipline instilled by her mother at a young age had never left her. She was used to feeling hungry but lately the cravings had got worse and she knew it made her irritable. She was likely to snap someone's head off and if that happened she was going to make sure the head belonged to the member of the Corretti family responsible for her current discomfort.

She'd wondered if he'd had done it on purpose. This film was his baby. He'd probably briefed the designer to make sure no man could remove her dress and ruin her big comeback.

Zach was going to laugh when he saw her. She'd lived in jeans for so long and he'd never seen this side of her.

She'd stayed away from this for so long she'd forgotten how much she hated it. She hated the falseness, the agendas hidden behind air kissing and polished smiles.

Resisting the childlike temptation to bite her nails, she glanced at her slick manicure and was depressed to see her hand shaking.

She didn't dare hold a glass of champagne. She'd spill her drink on her dress. Or, worse, on someone else's dress and she knew how that would be interpreted.

Irritated with herself for caring what people thought, she dropped the phone into her bag.

It was pathetic to be reacting like this about something so trivial. The past couple of years had taught her what mattered in life. There were people out there with real problems and hers were all of her own making and all in the past.

She'd made bad decisions. Trusted people when she shouldn't have done, but she was a different person now. Given time, she'd prove it.

And that was what today was all about, of course.

She was supposed to prove it.

No mistakes. No spilled drinks, however innocent the reason.

It didn't matter if someone threw oil on the path in front of her, she wasn't allowed to slip.

This was the price she had to pay if she wanted her acting career back—and she wanted it desperately. Desperately enough to star in the publicity circus that was part of the job. This was the price she had to pay for doing what she loved.

The thought had her dragging her phone out of her bag again. 'Hey, Zach?' Her voice shook. 'Just letting you know that the women here are really hot. Even you can't fail to get laid so hurry up before you miss your chance. And if that isn't enough to get you here then I can tell you that I can't pee unless someone removes the stitches from my dress. You are going to laugh yourself sick when you see me. Call, will you?'

She was frightened by how much she needed him here.

Zach was the one who had encouraged her to follow her dream and return to acting, but some dreams came with nightmares attached. If she couldn't cope with this, how was she going to be able to cope with the attention of being back on a film set? She missed acting, but she didn't miss this.

'Taylor!' Santo Corretti, head of the film production company who was reputed to have slept with every single leading lady of his past five films, strode towards her across the perfectly manicured grass. 'You're late.'

'I was being sewn into the dress you chose.' She didn't mention that she'd been outside for half an hour trying to summon the courage to walk through the gates. That was too embarrassing to admit to anyone. She was terrified he'd see through her perfectly groomed exterior to the shivering wreck beneath. 'In my experience the paparazzi are all the keener if you make them wait and work for it.'

'Just remember you're here to promote my film, not yourself. I want publicity and when I say publicity I mean good publicity. I don't want anyone raking up your past.'

There it was. Just two minutes into a conversation and already the topic was her 'past.'

There was no escaping it. Her mistakes had been played out so publicly they were branded into her so that now it was the first thing people saw, including him.

Her stomach growled a reminder that it was empty. 'In a wedding packed full of various members of the Corretti dynasty, I'm sure the press will have plenty of alternative headline options.' A different version of Taylor might have found him attractive but these days she avoided trouble instead of seeking it out. And she especially avoided the type of trouble that came shaped like a man. She'd learned that lesson and she'd learned it well.

'Are you blushing?' His eyes raked her face. 'Taylor Carmichael, wild child and sex kitten, able to blush when the situation demands it. I'll take that as a sign of your acting abilities. And I approve. The public loves vulnerability. They might even be prepared to excuse your shocking past.'

'My past is no one's business but my own.' But it was stuck to her, like a dirty mark she couldn't rub out. 'So who do you want me to charm first?'

'Weren't you bringing someone?' His eyes scanned the immediate area and Taylor managed to turn clenched teeth into a smile.

'My friend Zach, but he's been held up.' And she was going to kill him.

'Just remember your job today is to mingle with the people who matter, not nurture your love life.'

'Zach isn't—' She stopped in mid-sentence, wishing she'd stayed silent but already he was nodding approval.

'Good, because your messy love life has no place on my film set.'

'My love life isn't messy.' She could have told him her love life was non-existent but she didn't.

'There are two reasons this film is going to pull in a big audience. The first is because it's my film—' his smile was cool '—and the second is because you're starring in it, Taylor Carmichael. People are going to pack out movie theatres to see your big comeback because you're a train wreck and everyone loves ogling a train wreck. If I'm right about you, they'll leave knowing you can act. Don't screw up.'

Despite the heat, she shivered.

This was what she hated. The press intrusion and studios

who believed they owned her, not just on set, but in every area of her life. As a young star it had almost broken her, but she wasn't that naive girl any more.

There was no way she'd let that happen to her again.

There was no way she'd screw it up or let them screw her.

They could fix their damn camera lenses to her ass and they still wouldn't be able to catch her misbehaving. She was going to be so perfect the press would die of boredom. She was going to rub that dirty mark off her image until she shone like silver in sunshine.

'So who is the most important person here today? Give me a brief.' Brisk and professional, she was all business despite the fact the dress was all Hollywood. 'Who am I supposed to impress?'

'All of them. Every guest at the wedding is waiting for the chance to talk to you. Taylor Carmichael, finally back from exile. Everyone wants to know the details. The grapevine is buzzing.'

'You've made sure of it.'

'You're my biggest asset and I know how to use my assets. Don't give them details. No interviews until I say so.'

'No problem.' She'd pushed her past into a drawer and locked it and she hadn't opened that drawer for years. The thought that others might be trying to uncover her secrets made her feel sick and his next words didn't help dispel that feeling.

'They'll be persistent. After all, you're the girl who fired her own mother.'

'I fired my manager. The fact that she was my mother had nothing to do with it.' But it should have done. It shouldn't have been that easy to get rid of a mother, should it?

'People have a morbid fascination with the way you crashed your own life.'

'Thanks.' The pain rose and she pushed it down again, alone with it as she was always alone.

'So what have you been doing the past few years?'

Taylor watched as a bee hovered over a flower and then carefully landed on the fragile petals. 'I was keeping a low profile.'

His eyes narrowed at her evasive answer. 'Just as long as that profile isn't going to suddenly pop up and hurt my movie.'

'It won't.' She shifted her weight to ease the pain in her feet. She'd forgotten how uncomfortable stilettos were. Still, at least it took her mind off her growling stomach. 'You can relax. If there is any scandal attached to your movie, it won't come from me.'

'It's your first public appearance since you disappeared.' His tone was hard. 'Everyone is waiting for you to slip up, you know that, don't you?'

'Then I predict they're going to have a very boring time.'

'No drinking.'

'Is that why you had me sewn into the dress? So I can't use the bathroom?'

'The dress shows your body. Your body is one of your assets.'

There had to be some benefit for being permanently starving. 'And there was me hoping you wanted my acting skills.' The bitterness leaked into her voice and he narrowed his eyes.

'I do, but I'm not so naive as to think your looks don't help. It's all about the film, Carmichael. Don't answer any questions about the past. You are the Mona Lisa. All they get is an enigmatic smile.'

'I can tell you now there is no way Mona would have smiled if she were sewn into her dress. If she were forced to wear what I'm wearing she would have been the Moaning Lisa. And now we've established the ground rules, point me towards hell.'

'Wait. You didn't answer my question—' He caught her arm. 'What have you been doing with yourself for the past two years? You just disappeared. Were you in rehab or something?'

Rehab.

Of course they would think that. It never occurred to anyone that there could be any other explanation for her absence.

'Sorry,' Taylor murmured, disengaging her arm from his grip, 'I'm absolutely not permitted to talk about my past. Your rules.'

'You're a beautiful woman. There won't be any shortage of men interested, not in you but in the potential to make some money from selling a story. You screwed that up before.'

The pain was so intense he might as well have punched her. 'I was young. Trusting. I'm not any more. And as for men—' Taylor managed a careless shrug '—I can assure you there isn't a man out there hot enough to tempt me.'

Luca Corretti downed another glass of champagne to numb the boredom of behaving well.

For the past twenty-four hours he'd driven under the speed limit for the first time in his life, declined seven party invitations and made it to bed before dawn. The fact that he hadn't been alone at the time didn't count. As far as the outside world was concerned, his behaviour had been impeccable. The only thing he hadn't done in his quest for instant respectability was kissed a baby and even he wasn't prepared to descend to those levels of hypocrisy just to impress the board of directors who'd decided his lifestyle wasn't compatible with running another chunk of the family business. Apparently business flare counted for nothing, he thought savagely, wondering whether he could get away with swapping the champagne for whisky.

And now, to add insult to injury, he was expected to sit through his cousin's wedding.

Was he the only person who hated weddings? All that happy-ever-after crap that everyone knew was a temporary illusion. Or maybe it was a delusion. Luca didn't know and he didn't intend to find out. He was going to be out of here at the first opportunity, preferably with the brunette bridesmaid he'd spotted on his way in.

'Luca! I've been looking everywhere for you. Where have you been?'

Before he could react, Luca was enveloped in soft bosom and a choking cloud of perfume. At any other time he would have thought it wasn't a bad way to die, but he was conscious that heads were turning and, when heads turned, disapproval was bound to follow. It irritated him that he had to care. 'Where have I been?' He disentangled himself. 'Avoiding you, Penny.'

'My name's Portia.'

'Seriously? No wonder I didn't remember it.'

She giggled. 'You are a wicked, wicked man.'

'So people keep telling me.' Luca put down his empty glass, trying to think of a method of stress reduction that didn't involve sex or alcohol.

Portia lowered her eyelashes. 'About last night—'

Aware that his one indiscretion was about to be made public, Luca removed the drink from her hand and swapped it for orange juice. 'Last night? I have no idea what you're talking about. Last night I went to bed with a book.'

She gave a snort of laughter. 'Well, you certainly turned my pages. I'll never forget it. How could I?' Her eyes on his mouth, she leaned towards him. 'You were amazing. It's never been like that for me before. You're a genius.'

'So I keep telling the board,' Luca said in a flat drawl. 'Unfortunately my opinion doesn't seem to count. For some reason they seem to think activity in the bedroom saps my mental abilities so for the time being I have to prove I can keep my pants zipped.'

'We could be discreet. Leave the wedding.'

'I love weddings and I love my cousin,' Luca said immediately. 'I couldn't possibly leave until he's married…married—' what the hell was her name? '—the woman of his dreams.'

'You love weddings? Honestly?'

'Weddings never fail to make me cry,' Luca said truthfully. 'The thought of two people promising to love each other for ever makes me want to break down and sob like a baby.'

'Oh. I had no idea you were so romantic.' Her eyes misted. 'And I'm so pleased that all those rumours that you hate your cousins are wrong. You're nowhere near as bad as everyone says.'

'Bad?' Luca adopted his hurt expression. 'I'm a saint compared to some people.' He hoped she didn't ask him to name someone as bad as him because he knew he'd struggle.

'You're quite a softie—' she stroked his arm with her fingertips '—except in the one area that counts.' She'd moved closer to him again and Luca stood up, cursing his lack of thought in picking up a guest at the wedding.

What he'd taken to be a few moments of fun, she'd taken to be a future.

Now he had to shake her off before the Corretti board gave him another black mark.

Unfortunately Portia didn't want to be shaken anywhere. 'Will I see you tonight, after the wedding?'

'The definition of a one-night stand, *angelo mia*, is that it lasts one night.'

'You were keen enough last night.' She pouted. 'What's wrong? Don't you like me in this dress?' The words robbed him of breath.

Do I look good, Luca? Do I look better than her? Will he love me if I wear this?

'Luca?'

He dragged himself out of the black pit of his past and stared into Portia's over-made-up eyes. 'You look great,' he said flatly, relieved when one of the wedding guests shrieked a greeting and Portia was reluctantly dragged away.

Relieved by his narrow escape, he was momentarily distracted by a sheet of blonde hair that hung down the back of a woman standing on the far side of the terrace. People were pressing close, all desperate to get a piece of her, and he shifted slightly to see who she was.

When she finally turned her head, he felt a flash of surprise.

Taylor Carmichael. Well, well.

It cheered him up to know that there was one person present whose reputation was as bad as his.

According to the media, she'd done it all—drink, drugs and partying. And then she'd disappeared for a couple of years. He wondered what she'd been doing with herself and decided it was probably something disreputable. She was one of the few people at this wedding who could make him look saintly. Almost.

Luca watched her across the room and remembered reading that his cousin Santo had recruited her to play the lead in his latest film.

She had the most incredible body. Thinking that all that blonde hair would look good spread over his pillow, he took a step towards her and then remembered that members of the board were watching his every move and waiting for him to step out of line.

Exercising a restraint he didn't know he possessed, Luca turned away and engaged a suited man in a conversation about the economy.

If Taylor had been able to take a big enough breath, she would have screamed.

'You poor thing,' the woman said in a voice sweet enough to rot teeth. 'This wedding must be so stressful for you.'

'Why would it be stressful?' Taylor kept her smile in place

and wished Zach would show up. She was going to need someone to lend her a jacket when her stupid dress split. 'It's the perfect opportunity to meet interesting people.' *Unfortunately you're not one of them.*

'But so much temptation for someone like you.' The woman eyed the glass of water in Taylor's hand. 'I suppose you don't dare even take a sip of champagne in case you undo all the good work and lose control. It must be impossibly hard given the circle you move in.'

'It isn't hard.'

'What stops you drinking?'

The knowledge that she couldn't pee without the assistance of a seamstress. 'I'm going to be filming twelve hours a day. My focus is on my work.' And she couldn't wait. She knew that once she was playing that role, she'd be lost in it. Acting was all she wanted to do. And not just because it meant she could escape the empty, meaningless circus of her life.

Another woman pressed closer. 'I can't believe you're back in circulation. You just vanished off the face of the earth. You have to tell us whether those stories about you were true.'

They circled her like wolves waiting to pounce on a carcass. And she was the carcass.

Taylor laughed inwardly. Given the amount of weight she'd lost in preparation for this part, she almost *was* a carcass.

The moment filming was over she was going to rush to the nearest Dunkin' Donuts and indulge her carb fantasy but until then she had to play the game.

She couldn't keep this up for much longer. She was going to punch someone, split her dress and end up naked.

Exhausted, Taylor pressed a button on her phone and made it ring. 'Oh, excuse me—' with an apologetic smile, she pulled it out of her bag '—I just have to take this call. So good to meet you. I'll see you inside the chapel in a little while!' *And I hope you both choke on a canapé.*

Phone held to her ear, talking to herself in a bright tone,

she walked to the edge of the terrace, aware of Santo's eyes watching her every move.

As far as she was concerned, he could watch all he liked. She wasn't going to slip up.

She could do this. All she needed was a quick breather and then she'd sit somewhere at the back of the church, away from all the intrusive questions.

Bypassing the groups of people gathered on the terrace, she glanced around her to find somewhere less populated. Spying the English garden and, beyond that, the maze, she increased her pace. Perfect. What better place than a maze to find shade and peace?

The high hedges gave much-needed protection from the burning Sicilian heat and the curious stares of the other guests. Taylor slipped off her shoes, moaning with relief as the soft grass cooled her throbbing feet. Breathing deeply, she listened to the sound of the birds. Live in the moment, wasn't that what Zach had taught her? Block everything else out. It's all about now.

Slowly, her pulse rate slowed. The knot in her stomach eased, leaving only the hunger pangs that had been her constant companion since she'd signed up for the role. She was just congratulating herself on being back in control when she turned a corner and walked straight into a man.

'*Cristo*, can't you take a hint?' Hard hands gripped her and kept her on her feet but his tone was ice cold and Taylor stared at him, disorientated.

'What hint?' She recognised him instantly. Luca Corretti, billionaire playboy, occasionally described as Sicily's biggest tourist attraction and absolutely the last man in the world she would have chosen to be alone with given her current objective of staying out of trouble.

'*Mi dispiace, chicca.*' His smile was disturbingly attractive. 'I thought you were someone else.'

'Well, I'm not,' Taylor said coldly, 'so if you'd just let go of me, I can carry on walking and you can carry on hiding or whatever it is you're doing.'

'I'm dodging my past.'

Him too? 'I would have thought that was an ambitious objective for someone with your reputation.'

'Actually, I was talking about my immediate past. Last night.' His smile held no hint of apology. 'And you're not exactly in a position to judge, are you, Taylor Carmichael? Your past is every bit as dirty as mine.'

His use of her name made her insides lurch. 'You know who I am.'

'Of course. I've even seen you semi-naked.' Those eyes gleamed dangerously. 'That movie about the teenage runaway? God, you were sexy.'

Why did he have to pick that movie? She'd made over twenty films, but he'd picked the one she'd filmed at the very lowest point of her life.

She felt cold and hot at the same time. 'That was a long time ago.'

'But you have the same incredible legs....' His voice was a soft, sexy purr and his eyes dropped to her breasts. 'And other parts of you. I remember envying the director—what was his name? Rafaele. He got to see you on and off set, lucky bastard.'

Taylor felt as if someone was choking her. 'I don't want to talk about him.'

'Why not? So you dumped him and he sold his story to the press.' Luca gave a dismissive shrug. 'Who cares?'

She'd cared.

And she still cared.

She had no choice. The moment she'd accepted the film role, the texts had started. Just like before. It didn't matter how many times she changed her number, he always managed to track her down. His threats had been part of her life for nine years. Occasionally he went quiet, only to re-emerge when she'd started to hope it had all gone away and he'd finally become bored with tormenting her.

The dress was squeezing her like a boa constrictor trapping its prey. Taylor couldn't breathe. She tried desperately to change the subject. 'So what does your immediate past look like? Blonde? Brunette? You'd better tell me so that I can give her a wide berth. I'm not in the mood for dealing with an angry, jealous woman.'

'Me neither. Why the hell do you think I'm hiding in here?' He gave an exaggerated shudder and glanced up at the green wall of the maze. 'I'm hoping the Corretti board don't have security cameras planted round the grounds. I'm supposed to be behaving myself.'

Despite her stress, she found herself wanting to smile. 'This is what you're like when you're behaving yourself?'

'I'm positively restrained and it's killing me. Especially right this moment.' His eyes lingered on her mouth with blatant interest. 'I might be about to fall from the wagon. Or roll in the back of the wagon. You and me. Together. Now there's an interesting thought.'

Taylor felt her heart beat faster.

Against her will, her eyes moved to his mouth too. Firm, sensual and very masculine. There was no doubt in her mind that Luca Corretti would be a skilled kisser. If rumour were correct, he'd certainly had enough practice.

Appalled by her own thoughts, she turned her head away and took a step backwards. 'It's a thought that doesn't interest me in the slightest. I'll leave you to hide. I hope your past doesn't catch up with you.'

'Me too. I don't suppose you saw her on your way in?'

'I didn't see anyone. What does she look like?'

'Desperate?'

She choked back a laugh. 'You spent the night with her?'

'Not the whole night, obviously.' He looked so horrified by the suggestion that this time she did laugh.

'Have you ever spent the whole night with a woman?'

'*Cristo*, no! My mantra is "Until dawn us do part." My longest commitment so far is six hours and I was bored by the end of that. You?'

It was uncomfortable to remember the number of times she'd thought a man was serious about her only to discover he was only interested in selling her out to the press. It had been a harsh training ground for independence. 'I'm not big on romantic commitment.'

He groaned. 'You should not have told me that.'

'Why?'

'Because that makes you my perfect woman.' That sexy mouth slanted into a charismatic smile. 'Just don't tell me you're addicted to sex and fast cars or I'm doomed.'

Silence stretched between them. They were standing in the dappled shade of the maze but the heat was stifling and oppressive.

Their eyes met and held.

His head lowered towards hers.

And suddenly they heard voices.

Appalled by how close they'd come to kissing, she glanced at him only to find him doubled up with laughter.

Taylor was torn between laughter and panic. The last thing she needed was to be caught with Luca Corretti. No one would believe it was an innocent encounter.

'Stop panicking, *angelo mia*, I'll rescue you.' Putting his finger to his lips, Luca took her hand in his and forced her to sprint with him deeper into the maze. 'I am the expert at the great escape. No one knows more about running from women than I do.'

'What are you doing? I don't want to be caught running away with you. And don't pull me—this dress has no give in it.' She tugged at her hand but he held it firmly, turned another corner and she gave a little gasp because there, in a shaded glade, was a pretty fountain and by the fountain was an open bottle of champagne.

'No glasses, I'm afraid.' With a wicked, sexy smile he released her hand and retrieved the bottle. 'We'll have to slum it.'

Weak with relief that they'd avoided detection, Taylor shook her head in disbelief as she watched him. 'How did you—?'

'How did I get it here?' Those wide shoulders lifted in a careless shrug. 'I imported it here under cover of darkness in case of emergencies. This definitely constitutes an emergency. Judging from the look on your face earlier, your need is as great as mine. I'm always willing to help out a fellow sinner in need. Sit down. Make yourself comfortable. Take a dip in the cool water.'

Taylor looked wistfully at the fountain. 'I wish I could. This dress is the most uncomfortable thing I've ever worn but sadly it isn't designed to allow sitting.'

'So take it off.'

'Even if I wanted to, I couldn't. They've sewn me into it.' She caught his look of astonishment and glared. 'Don't ask.'

'All right—' there was laughter in his eyes '—but if you want my opinion I'd say you've been stitched up, *angelo mia*.'

'Very funny.'

'I like the idea that you're sewn into your dress. It could be erotic.' He prowled around her, his eyes on her body. 'So what do they expect you to do if you need to have wild, animal sex?'

'I'm not going to need that.'

He scanned her dress. 'This is your punishment for not picking something from the House of Corretti. Our clothes would make you feel seductive and feminine. We don't have to sew our women into their dresses for them to look good. The dress becomes part of the woman.'

She'd forgotten that he ran the fashion house but it explained his effortlessly stylish appearance. Even with his shirt collar open and strands of dark hair falling over his forehead, he looked spectacular.

'I didn't pick this dress.' Heat and hunger made her irritable. 'I wore what your cousin told me to wear.'

'He'd never pick anything from my company,' Luca drawled, 'it might signify approval and God forbid the rivalry between us should ever die. That fabric isn't allowing your body to breathe. I could help you with that.'

'Nice try.'

'I've got moves that would make you weep.'

'I'm sure you make women weep a lot, but I'm not a crier.'

'I like you more and more. You could bathe naked in the fountain.' He reached for the chilled bottle of champagne. 'Or I could roll this over your skin.'

Her skin was prickling with the heat and she made a sound that was half laugh, half groan. 'Now you're torturing me. Talk about something else, before I melt.' Taylor knew she should walk away but she decided it was safer to wait a few minutes until the people they'd overheard were safely back among the guests. Just five minutes, she promised herself. Five minutes. 'So who is this woman you're running from?'

'I have no idea. Apparently her name is Portia but that was news to me.'

Taylor lifted her hair away from her neck to try and cool herself down. 'You're terrible.'

'Not terrible enough to induce her to dump me, sadly. She was alarmingly difficult to shift.'

'Some women find bad boys attractive.'

'And from what I've heard, you know a lot about that.'

'Do you often listen to gossip?'

'All the time. Gossip makes me laugh.' The cork flew out of the bottle with a pop. 'So tell me the truth, Taylor Carmichael? How do you like your men? Well-done, medium or rare?'

'Rare.' Sticky and uncomfortable from the heat and the conversation she squirmed, wishing she could dip her toes in the water. 'So rare I can't remember when I last touched one.'

'So I'm looking at a desperate woman.'

'You're looking at a controlled woman. I'm no longer a slave to my impulses.'

'That sounds like the tag line for a good bondage movie. Slave to Her Impulses. The sequel could be Slave to His Impulses. I might be willing to star in that for a price providing you were the leading lady.' That mocking smile touched the corners of his mouth and he tipped champagne into a glass and held it out to her. 'Drink. It will help numb the boredom of the wedding.'

Hating the fact that she was even tempted, Taylor reluctantly shook her head. 'No, thanks. Champagne is on my list of banned substances, particularly on an empty stomach.'

'Personally I have a taste for banned substances.' Shrugging, he tilted his head and drank, the sun glinting off his dark hair.

Just for a moment, because he wasn't looking at her, she looked at him. At those slanting cheekbones, that nose, the olive skin—

It was so long since she'd looked at a man and found him attractive, the spasm of sexual awareness shocked her.

She reminded herself that Luca Corretti was probably the most dangerous man she could possibly have found herself with. 'I thought you were trying to behave yourself.'

'This is me behaving myself.' He took another mouthful of champagne and she laughed in spite of herself, sensing a kindred spirit. A part of her long buried stirred to life.

'So both of us are making a superhuman effort to behave. What's your excuse?'

'I have to prove myself capable of taking charge of another chunk of the family business.' Underneath the light, careless tone there was an edge of steel and it surprised her because she didn't associate him with responsibility.

That thought was followed instantaneously by guilt. She was judging him as others judged her, based on nothing but gossip. She was better than that.

'But you already run a business. I read that you'd turned the House of Corretti around.'

'I have a flare for figures.'

'Especially when those figures belong to models?'

He laughed. 'Something like that. Unfortunately trebling the profits of Corretti isn't enough for them.'

She had to stop herself reaching for the champagne in his hand. Because she wasn't able to get out of her dress, she'd avoided drinking and now her throat was parched from the heat. 'But why do you want to meddle in other parts of the business?'

'Sibling rivalry.'

'But you're all members of the same family. Surely that qualifies you for a seat on the board.'

'The qualifications for a seat on the board seem to be old age and sexual inactivity.' He suppressed a yawn. 'I suppose that's why they call it a "bored." Needless to say I'm bombing out big-time. I have a feeling that whatever I do, I will always be in the wrong.'

Taylor felt a flicker of sympathy. 'I know that feeling.'

'I'm sure you do. You, Taylor Carmichael, are one, big walking wrong.' His gaze lingered on her mouth. 'So tell me what else is on your list of banned substances.'

'Men like you.'

'Is that right?' His eyes on hers, he lowered the champagne bottle back into the fountain. Somehow, without her even noticing how he'd done it, he'd moved closer to her. His dark head was between her and the sun and all she could see was those wicked eyes tempting her towards the dark side.

'What are you doing?'

'Testing a theory.' His mouth moved closer to hers and suddenly she struggled to breathe.

'What theory?'

'I want to know whether two wrongs make a right.' His smile was the last thing she saw before he kissed her.

CHAPTER TWO

WHAT THE HELL was she doing?

Taylor opened her eyes and found herself staring into two dark, slumberous pools of molten male hunger.

As his mouth moved skilfully on hers, desire punched low in her belly and then spread through her body with a speed that shocked her. One minute she was thinking, the next minute she was kissing him back, gripped by a deep, visceral emotion she couldn't even name.

He seduced her mouth with lazy expertise, his tongue teasing hers with a delicious skill that weakened her legs with frightening speed.

Her stomach twisted. Her body melted. She wanted to stretch luxuriously into the warmth of that hand resting high on her bare thigh.

Her bare thigh?

Horrified, she tried to pull back but her body was weakened by pleasure. 'My dress—' The words were swallowed by the heat of his mouth. 'Luca—'

'I agree. The dress has to come off.'

'No.' She was laughing and appalled at the same time, her hand covering his as she stopped him sliding the fabric upwards. 'You've ripped the stitches.'

'No, you ripped the stitches,' he purred, 'when you wrapped your leg around me.'

'You pulled my leg round you—we shouldn't be doing this. I don't want to be doing this.'

'Tell that to your pulse rate. It's revving like the engine of my Ferrari.'

'I thought you were trying to prove to the board you're responsible?'

'I'll use a condom. Does that count?'

Appalled by how much she wanted to laugh, Taylor locked her hand in the front of his shirt, feeling hard male muscle against the backs of her fingers. 'I don't think that's what they have in mind. You don't want to take this risk and neither do I. We have to get back to the wedding before the bride comes.'

'If I have my way you'll come before the bride.' Laughing wickedly, he delivered a slow, sensual kiss to the corner of her mouth. 'Some things are worth taking a risk for and you, Taylor Carmichael, are definitely one of those. You are sexy enough to make me forget all about being good—' his hand was buried in her hair and his mouth was on her neck '—and it really turns me on to know that underneath your icy, composed exterior you are still a bad, bad girl.'

Taylor closed her eyes but that simply intensified the crazy swirl of feelings so she opened them again. 'You're wrong. That isn't who I am.' It couldn't be. 'I don't want this.'

'You're crushing me, *dolcezza*.' He was kissing her jaw and she could hear the smile in his voice. 'Think of my poor, delicate ego.'

Nothing about him was delicate. Not the powerful shoulders, nor the rock-hard biceps. He was all muscle and masculinity and Taylor was so desperate for him her whole body ached. 'I don't want you.'

'Yes, you do. You want me as much as I want you but you're determined to deny your true self.'

'I'm not denying anything.' Panicking, she shoved at his chest. 'Enough! Damn it, Luca—get away from me.' In the past two years she hadn't even looked at a man and suddenly here she was, pressed against the hardness of him, her body melting against the heat of his. The chemistry was off the scale and it terrified her. Of all the men she could have found herself with, he was the most dangerous of his species. 'I'm not that person any more. I've changed.'

'That person? What person? You mean the woman who embraced her life without apology?'

'The woman who screwed up her life by trusting men like you,' Taylor snapped, 'and I'm not doing it again so stay away. I mean it, Luca. If you want to live up to your reputation then go ahead, but I'm not going to let you take me down with you.'

'Why are you so ashamed of yourself?'

'I'm not ashamed—' she spoke so quickly she stumbled over the words '—but I've grown up.'

'Grown-ups accept their mistakes instead of running from them.'

Hers haunted her.

The threatening messages never ended.

Her heart was pumping as she backed away from him. 'Good luck with your future. I hope you manage to convince the board to trust you before you give in to the worst part of yourself and blow it completely.'

'Ah, but that's the difference between us, *angelo mia.*' Reaching for the bottle of champagne again, he leaned his hips against the fountain, effortlessly sophisticated and insanely sexy. 'I consider it to be the best part of myself. The fact that no one else appreciates it is their problem, not mine.'

For a brief moment she felt a flash of envy that he was so indifferent to what people thought and then the urgency of her situation propelled her into action and she jammed her feet into her shoes, the movement parting the seam of her dress as far as the waist. Gripping it with her hand, she held the two sides together and hurried through the shadowed corridors of the maze, grateful for the high hedges that concealed her from prying eyes.

If a photographer had been hiding in the maze, or even another guest—one of Luca's disgruntled women—it would have looked awful and no amount of explaining would have worked.

She would have ruined everything before she'd even started filming.

The thought of how close she'd come to doing just that made her feel sick.

Weak with relief that her reputation was still intact, she pulled her phone out of her bag and texted the designer one-handed.

Ready to be sewn back into my dress. Meet me by the maze.

Luca let her go, that exercise in self-restraint costing him dearly in terms of physical discomfort. He shifted slightly and decided he didn't dare leave the maze until his hormones had settled down.

Lifting the champagne to his lips, he paused as he spotted a woman approaching down another green-lined tunnel.

'Luca, there you are!'

Cursing under his breath, he lowered the bottle of champagne. 'Paula!'

'It's Portia.'

'That's what I said. The maze distorts sound.'

Her eyes were a little less warm than they'd been earlier. 'Were you hiding from me?'

'I didn't trust myself around you,' Luca said smoothly. With the taste of Taylor still on his lips, he felt no inclination to take her up on her less than subtle invitation. 'Last night should not have happened. You're a beautiful woman but I need to behave myself.'

Her eyes narrowed and she stared down the path where Taylor had recently disappeared. 'Really? So you're telling me women are off the agenda today?'

Something in her tone made Luca wonder if she'd seen

Taylor but he decided that wasn't possible. No one could have sneaked up on them without him noticing.

'Sadly, yes. What we shared was very special—' he pulled out one of his stock phrases '—but I can't risk anything else at this point which is killing me because last night was one of the best of my life.'

'All right. If that's the way it has to be then so be it.' She looked at him for a long moment, as if she were working something out. 'You're never going to forget me, Luca Corretti.'

'Of course I'm not.'

'And you'll never again forget my name.'

'It's your own fault for being beautiful—I take one look at your face and my memory goes.'

Three minutes, Luca thought idly, glancing to the place he'd last seen Taylor and missing the jealous glint in the woman's eye. That was how long it would take him to forget her.

Forty-eight hours later Taylor sat in the back of a limo as she was driven to the docklands for filming to begin. She'd spent the entire previous day locked in her hotel room checking every online newspaper and gossip column for pictures, terrified that her momentary lapse with Luca might have been captured on camera. When she realised she'd got away with it she'd been weak with relief.

From now on she was going to keep well away from men like Luca Corretti.

Never again would she do something that gave a man power over her.

But even as she thought that, she knew that her response hadn't been driven by stupidity but by a raw attraction so strong nothing could have prepared her for it.

And it wasn't just his physical appeal that had caused her downfall, it had been something else. Something layered beneath the surface of masculine perfection. An honesty that presented a stark contrast to the atmosphere of falseness that had hovered over the wedding. Yes, that was it. Luca Corretti embraced everything he was. He took what he wanted without explanation or apology and that was—she struggled to describe it—refreshing.

She felt a twinge of envy and dismissed it instantly. She didn't want to be like Luca, a slave to her emotions. Her life had been so much happier since she'd been in control.

'We'll be there in ten minutes, Miss Carmichael.'

The voice of her driver came through the intercom and excitement buzzed through her. She couldn't wait to be back on a film set. She was going to throw herself into her work and forget about her narrow escape. And forget about Luca.

Blocking out disturbing memories of that kiss, Taylor leaned her head back against the seat, finally able to think back to the wedding and laugh. What a crazy day. She still couldn't believe that Luca's brother Matteo had run off with the bride before she'd made it as far as the altar. Bad behaviour was obviously in the DNA, but she was grateful for that because all the attention that had been focused on her had immediately switched to the Corretti family.

She shook her head at the irony of it.

And Santo Corretti had been worried about her causing a scandal.

As the car approached the docklands area, she noticed the pack of photographers pressed against the security fence and her heart sank.

There were so many of them, no doubt all waiting for her to screw up on her first day and give them a nice juicy headline.

Was it going to be like this all the time?

Her phone buzzed with a text and she checked it quickly, her heart rate doubling when she saw it was from Rafaele.

New phone. New number. And still he had no trouble contacting her.

She hesitated and then opened the text.

Good luck today. Enjoy Sicily.

Flinging the phone back in her bag, she rubbed her forehead with fingers that shook. She felt as if she'd been dipped in iced water. He wasn't wishing her luck, he was telling her that he knew exactly what she was doing and where she was doing it.

She was never going to be rid of him. Never.

Knowing that she couldn't afford to think of him now, she took a deep breath as the car slowed and shut off all those parts of herself she no longer showed to the world. Maybe everyone at the wedding had been fake, but she was the biggest fake of all. No one saw the real Taylor. She hadn't even been sure she could access the real Taylor any more until that moment in the maze with Luca.

Pushing that thought aside, she stepped out of the car, telling herself that the media attention would die down after the first day of filming.

Her confidence lasted as long as it took her to notice the black expression on the director's face. She'd assumed he was meeting her in person out of courtesy and respect for her position on the movie, but one look at his face told her that was a false assumption.

It was a struggle to keep her smile steady. 'Sorry about the media circus. Hopefully they'll lose interest soon enough.'

'Why would they lose interest when you are a never-ending source of juicy stories?' His voice was cold. 'Your brief was to create interest in the movie, not in your personal life. The moment Santo told me he wanted you on the project I knew it would be a disaster.'

'Oh.' Shaken by that unwelcome news, Taylor spun a few more layers of protection between her feelings and the world and kept it professional. 'I'd like to think you'd judge me on my performance now, not on something that happened years ago.'

'The whole world is judging you on your performance at the Corretti wedding.' His face was scarlet with anger and for the first time Taylor noticed the newspaper clutched in his hand.

'The wedding never happened, but even I couldn't be blamed for that, surely?' Confused, she eyed the newspaper. Did people even still buy those things? If she ever wanted to glance at headlines she just used her phone. 'If you're worried about the fact the wedding didn't go ahead, then don't be. I'm sure Santo Corretti will deal with it. The publicity might even be good for the film.'

His mouth opened and closed. '"Good" that the movie-going public see you as a man-stealer?'

She looked at him blankly. 'A what?'

'Just in case you were too drunk to know what you were doing, you can read it for yourself.'

Taylor almost lost her balance as he thrust the paper at her. 'I don't drink. And I remember everything.' An image of Luca's handsome face floated into her head and she pushed it away as she fumbled with the newspaper.

'Portia Bateman.' He enunciated every syllable. 'Are you going to tell me that name doesn't mean anything to you?'

'Yes, that's exactly what I'm going to tell you because it doesn't. I've never heard of Portia Bateman.' Taylor's mind was working in slow motion. Her fingers were clumsy as she unfolded the offending paper. 'In fact, I don't know a single person called Portia—' The words stuck in her mouth as a snippet of conversation rose in her mind.

So who is this woman you're hiding from?

Apparently her name is Portia.

Driven by a horrible, awful suspicion, she shook her head. 'Oh, no, no, she can't have done that. I checked. I looked…' She muttered the words to herself but the director was watching her keenly.

'So you do know someone called Portia.'

'No, I don't! I've never even met her. She's just someone he…' She scanned the piece, saw the photograph of a tearful blonde woman under the caption *Exclusive—Taylor Carmi-*

chael Stole My Man. And there beneath the caption was a photograph of her and Luca. His bronzed hand was plastered against her bare thigh and they were kissing. Not just kissing. Devouring each other. Passion was painted into every line of the photo and she stared at it in dismay.

Her fingers gripped the paper.

The sounds faded around her.

Dizziness washed over her.

She'd congratulated herself on the fact that no paparazzi had caught her moment of indiscretion. She'd forgotten that since the advent of camera phones, everyone was a photographer. And this one had hit the jackpot.

Bathed in horror, Taylor closed her eyes. This couldn't be happening to her. It just couldn't be. She couldn't think through the panic. 'Why did she wait a day to publish this?'

'She says she offered Luca Corretti the chance to buy the photograph but he just laughed and told her to go ahead and sell whatever story she wanted to print. So she did. She sold her story to the highest bidder.'

He'd laughed?

Taylor felt cold.

What had she done?

The answer to that was nothing, but no one looking at this photograph was going to believe that. She'd dropped her guard for a few moments, that was all, and this was the result.

Keeping her expression neutral, she handed the newspaper back to the glowering director. She wanted to wake up and start the day again. She wanted to wind the clock back. She wanted to never have gone to that damn wedding. Most of all she wanted to kick Luca Corretti in a place that would ensure he'd never seduce a woman again.

'I understand your concerns and I realise that the story looks bad, but I'm asking you to trust me. This piece isn't—' how on earth could she even begin to justify it in a way that would change his expression from sour to sympathetic?

'—accurate. Please judge me on my acting ability, not the media circus that follows me.'

'You think that pack of journalists are interested in your acting ability? Your movie comeback is over before it began. Santo Corretti is on his way here now and I can tell you he is not amused. After that wedding fiasco he isn't in the best of moods as it is and this project means a lot to him. He doesn't want it hijacked by your never-ending need to grab the headlines.'

He wasn't interested in an explanation, Taylor thought numbly. The truth wasn't going to help and a small part of her couldn't even blame him for that because the picture did look incriminating. It had just been a kiss. Other people kissed all the time and did a whole lot worse and no one knew or cared. She slipped for one moment and the evidence was plastered everywhere and she had her mother to thank for that. She'd ensured the media had been fed a steady diet of Taylor Carmichael from the first moment she'd stuck her child in front of the camera.

Taylor wondered if Luca had even seen the pictures.

He'd probably laugh, she thought bitterly. It wasn't his naked thigh that was up there for the world to see. It wasn't his career that was ruined. Even if the board refused to give him more responsibility, he still had the fashion house. And anyway, he didn't appear to care what the world thought of him. In fact, he seemed to behave in a way designed to invite and encourage salacious headlines.

'I can tell you that Luca Corretti isn't involved with that woman. It's a kiss and tell. He rejected her and she's getting her revenge.'

'So you're trying to tell me that picture is Photoshopped?'

'No, but—'

'It's not you he's kissing?'

'Yes, it's me, but—'

'It's not your dress that's ripped?'

'The dress isn't ripped. The stitches came undone.' Feeling like a fox with a pack of hungry hounds snapping at her heels, Taylor gritted her teeth. 'They sewed me into it which I knew was a stupid idea right from the start.'

The director looked disgusted. 'This story is everywhere. Tell me how I'm supposed to deal with this. How am I supposed to focus on making this movie when every single person on my set is looking at the bare thigh of my leading lady and sniggering? Just being this close to you is making me feel dirty.'

The whole world is going to know you're dirty, Taylor.

Her breathing grew shallow.

Anger burst free inside her. This was all Luca's fault. Because he didn't care what people thought of him, he'd exposed her. He'd stripped her, almost literally, with no thought to the consequences. If he hadn't been so careless with that Portia woman's feelings, this would never have happened.

'The press have embellished this to make it look bad, but it isn't how it seems.'

'The truth doesn't even matter.' The director made a hand gesture to signify two minutes to someone over her shoulder. 'I can't work in this circus. You're off the movie.'

Those words turned Taylor's limbs to water. 'What? No!' Composure deserted her. She wanted to act. More than anything else she wanted to act. It was all she wanted to do.

'You can't do that. You can't get rid of me because of what the media say. You can't give them that much power and control. I need to speak to Luca. Give me a chance to sort this out.'

But he'd already moved on. People were shouting things at him and his eyes were on the phone in his hand as he read a text. 'You can't sort this out. Wherever you go, trouble follows. It's always about you and never about the film. You're finished.'

Furious at the injustice of it, Taylor straightened her shoulders. 'That's Santo Corretti's decision, not yours.'

'Fine. He can tell you himself.' Standing back, the director gestured towards the low, expensive sports car that had just parked behind her.

Taylor closed her eyes. This was a nightmare. She had to do something but nothing she said was going to rub out that picture of Luca with his hand on her thigh.

She forced herself to stand still as Santo strode towards her, his face black as the sky before a storm.

Judging from the little she'd read about the aborted wedding, he'd had a worse weekend than she had.

'It isn't how it seems,' she said, trying and failing to keep the desperation out of her voice. Part of her hated herself for having to try and excuse herself but she was willing to do anything to keep the part. 'She's one of his exes and she obviously followed him and spied on him.'

'And what were you and Luca doing together in the first place?'

'I was—' She broke off, suddenly furious with Luca. If he'd just paid the woman they wouldn't be in this mess. Her mind raced ahead. She'd make him pay in another way. 'We were meeting each other. You told me I couldn't have a relationship, so we were trying to be discreet.'

'Luca is never discreet. He does exactly what he wants to do with whomever he wishes to do it. He doesn't care.'

'But I do, and he respected that. He understands what the press are like and he wanted to protect me.'

Santo shot her a look of undiluted incredulity. 'Your date at the wedding was some guy called Zach. I heard you on the phone.'

'And you heard me tell you that Zach isn't my boyfriend,' she said truthfully. 'He's just a friend.' And by that she meant that he was allowed one layer closer to the real her than most people.

The truth was she trusted no one.

'So you were using him to cover the fact that you're with Luca? You're trying to convince me that you and my cousin are an item?'

'That's exactly what I'm telling you.'

'My cousin isn't capable of a relationship.'

'I think he was as surprised by how quickly our relationship developed as I was. After what you said to me, I made him promise to keep it a secret. I couldn't change the way we felt about each other, but I thought I could stop you finding out. There is nothing sleazy about that kiss.' Making a last-ditch attempt to halt the free fall of her career, she shot a look at the director. 'It was two people sharing a special moment and that woman exploited that. We love each other. Now can we move on?'

'Love?' The director started to laugh. 'You expect us to believe that nonsense? Today it's Luca Corretti—who will it be tomorrow?' Perhaps if he hadn't sounded so contemptuous, she wouldn't have said it but she was so upset at his implication that she was unlovable, the words fell out of her mouth.

'It won't be anyone tomorrow,' Taylor heard herself say, 'because I'm in love with Luca and he's in love with me. We're getting married.' People used her all the time. Why shouldn't she use someone else for a change? And since this was all Luca's fault, he was the lucky candidate. 'We didn't want to say anything on Saturday and draw attention away from the bride and bridegroom.' She couldn't for the life of her remember their names. 'We were trying to be unselfish which is why we sneaked a quiet few minutes together.' For a few seconds she had the satisfaction of seeing the pair of them silenced. She held her breath, knowing that they were never going to believe her. Never.

Santo was the first to break the silence. 'If my cousin were engaged, I would have heard.'

'It's a secret.' So much of a secret that even Luca didn't know about it. Her insides clenched as she realised the enormity of what she'd done. 'No one knew but us. And because we're keeping it a secret, obviously we had to be discreet.' She snapped her mouth shut before she could trip over her own tangle of lies. 'And now I'd be grateful if neither of you would mention it again. As far as the media is concerned, I'm single. That's what you wanted, isn't it?'

The director let out a stream of profanities and raised the palms of his hands. 'I can't work with this. If you want me on this project, I demand another actress.'

Santo stood in silence, a frown on his brow.

Taylor felt sick. So that was it. It was all over. She was just about to slide back into her car and hide her humiliation behind tinted glass when Santo spoke.

'Taylor stays on this project.'

The director's eyes narrowed. 'If she stays, I go.'

'Then go.' With a total absence of sympathy, Santo nodded his head at Taylor. 'We'll talk to the press and then get on with the job we're here to do.'

'You just fired the director.' Stunned by his unexpected support, Taylor could hardly speak. 'And yesterday you told me to be discreet and not say anything to the press.'

'That was when I thought you were likely to stir up a scandal. Taylor Carmichael engaged to Luca Corretti isn't scandal, it's news. It will stop the media focusing on your past and it will shift attention away from my family's wedding fiasco. Don't look so shocked—' he placed the flat of his hand on her bag and guided her towards the press pack '—you've finally done something right. Relax, you still have a job.'

There were only two thoughts in her head. The first was that when Santo found out the truth, he'd fire her anyway, and the second was that Luca Corretti was going to kill her.

CHAPTER THREE

'I'VE BEEN CALLED before the board, no doubt to answer for my sins. This promises to be a gripping meeting, Jeannie, the general tone of which will be that I'm a very bad boy who can't possibly be trusted with the company even though my brother has just very inconveniently gone AWOL and another of my disgruntled cousins is trying to take over our flagship hotel.' Hiding his bitterness beneath layers of boredom, Luca leaned back and put his feet on his desk, earning himself a reproving look from his long-suffering PA.

'You could try not to be so shocking all the time.'

'Where would be the fun in that?'

'I'm just saying it might help if you were more...' She hesitated and he lifted an eyebrow to prompt her.

'More?'

'More conventional.'

'Conventional?' Just saying the word made Luca shudder. 'In the fashion business that word is death. And talking of death, whose idea was it to put lilies in my office? Get rid of them. They remind me of funerals.'

She put a strong cup of coffee in front of him and glanced at the extravagant display of fresh flowers that dominated the centre of the table he used for internal meetings. 'I'll have them changed. Gianni is having a meltdown. He wants to know if you've approved the location for the fashion shoot?

The agency is driving him mad. He wanted me to remind you the theme is nautical, using unexpected twists on classic elements.'

Luca rolled his eyes. 'Roughly translated from designer-speak to normal language, that means the sea, yes?'

'The agency wants to use your yacht but Gianni wants something more edgy.'

'I don't want them on my yacht. It's my bolt hole from press madness.'

'Talking of press madness, they've been calling all morning about your latest—' she cleared her throat '—indiscretion. Is there anything you want me to say to them?'

'Yes. You can tell them to mind their own business.' Irritated, Luca swung his legs off the desk. 'Don't look so shocked about it. You've worked for me for ten years. I know nothing shocks you.'

'I just get upset when I read bad things about you.' Jeannie's voice was fierce and Luca frowned slightly.

'Don't let it bother you. I don't.'

'That's why I let it bother me. One of us has to care, and it doesn't seem to be you. I could strangle that Portia woman with my bare hands. How dare she tell those terrible lies.'

'Ah, yes, Portia. I underestimated her.' He wondered how Taylor was coping with the publicity and then shrugged it off. If anyone was capable of dealing with a media feeding frenzy, it was Taylor Carmichael. Her past was almost as messy as his. 'The lawyers are dealing with it. I'm not worried.'

'I'm worried enough for both of us. Between you and your brother, you keep the media going—'

'Talking of my brother, I don't suppose anyone has heard from him since he ran off with the bride?' Shaking with laughter, Luca checked his phone for messages while Jeannie gave a despairing shake of her head.

'It isn't funny! What about poor Alessandro?'

'"Poor" Alessandro had a narrow escape. He's been saved

from a miserable marriage followed by an expensive divorce. He should be celebrating his good fortune.'

'You don't really think that.'

'I try to think about marriage as little as possible.'

'Your parents were married for years.'

Luca stilled. If there was one thing worse than thinking of marriage in general then it was thinking of his parents' marriage. 'Did I miss the memo about introducing boring topics into office conversation?'

'Sorry.' Jeannie flushed. 'But where do you think Matteo is?'

Luca shrugged. 'Holed up somewhere enjoying wild honeymoon sex with his cousin's almost-bride, I suppose, which makes it all the more galling that the board are proving so intransigent. They need a Corretti to run the company in his absence to stop that snake Angelo getting his claws on the company. They should be embracing me.'

'Judging from the pictures of you and Taylor Carmichael, they probably think there's been more than enough embracing.'

Taylor Carmichael.

He could still feel the silk of her hair against his fingers and the soft slide of her tongue against his mouth. In those few moments before she'd pushed him away, they'd created enough heat and energy to power a small country. The blaze of sexual chemistry had shocked him as much as her, the only difference was that he hadn't wanted to fight it.

Before he could respond to Jeannie, the phone on his desk rang and she leaned across to answer it.

'Signor Corretti's office—no, he is currently out of the office....Which rumour?' She paused, her calm professionalism visibly disintegrating as she listened to the person on the other end of the phone. She lifted shocked eyes to Luca. 'No, I don't have any comment to make....Yes, I'll tell him you rang.' Her hand shook as she replaced the phone and it immediately rang again. Luca clamped his hand over hers as she reached for it.

'Leave it—it's just the press wanting more details on that kiss. Don't feed the frenzy.'

'They didn't want details of the kiss.' Jeannie looked at him nervously. 'You're not the sort of guy who would shoot the messenger, are you?'

His radar for trouble on full alert, Luca released her hand and leaned back in his chair. 'That,' he drawled slowly, 'depends on the message.'

She swallowed hard. 'They want to know when you'll release a statement on your engagement.'

'I'm sure when he said that no one was to disturb him, he didn't mean me.' Taylor shot a dazzling smile at the security guard who was left blinded.

'Well, er, he hasn't mentioned you as such, Miss Carmichael—'

'Of course he hasn't. We agreed not to speak about each other.' She stepped closer and lowered her eyelashes just enough to ensure he wouldn't be able to think about anything but her all day. 'If he talked about me, our relationship wouldn't be a secret, would it?'

'I suppose not.' Sweating, he slid a finger around his collar. 'Knowing Mr Corretti, I'm sure he'll be only too pleased to see a beautiful woman walking into his office.'

'Good.' Striding into the express elevator before he could change his mind, Taylor hit a button and closed the doors. Safely inside, she switched off her megawatt smile and checked her reflection in the mirror.

She was going to kill the bastard.

First she was going to rip his elegant suit from his perfect body and then she was going to injure him in places that would ensure he'd remember her for ever.

It had proved difficult to persuade Santo to give her a

few hours off from filming, but in the end he'd decided that they'd be more productive if they dealt with the media first.

Taylor hadn't revealed that the only person she was going to be 'dealing with' was Luca.

The doors opened and Taylor stepped out into a contemporary office space like no other she'd seen. The walls were lined with photographs. Famous models in various poses pouted at her, their razor-sharp cheekbones accentuated by the powerful beam of sunlight pouring from an atrium above. It was a shrine to beauty and elegance.

The wide glass reception desk was unoccupied and she looked through the open door beyond and saw Luca Corretti at the same moment he saw her.

Their eyes locked.

Just for a moment she was back in the maze with his hand pressed to her bare thigh but then she remembered that was the reason she was here and her temper spurted.

'Well, well—' his sarcastic drawl carried across the open space between them '—it's my fiancée. What an unexpected pleasure, *angelo mia*.'

'In the circumstances, how could I stay away?' Head held high, in full battle mode, Taylor stalked across the marble floor and into his office wondering how on earth they were going to unpick this mess.

She was going to kill him and how was she going to explain that to the press?

'Leave us, Jeannie,' Luca ordered in a silky tone. 'It's not every day a man gets engaged. I need to savour the moment. I might even indulge in desk sex so better not come in without knocking.'

The woman sent him a troubled look and then retreated from the office and closed the door behind her.

Taylor went straight into attack mode. 'How dare you? How dare you play with my life just because you don't care about yours! You should have paid that woman.'

'If I paid every woman who threatened to take stories of me to the press I'd be broke.'

'Maybe you should stop seducing women and then the problem would go away!' She paced the length of his office, her attention caught by yet more black-and-white photographs on the walls. 'You have photographs of women everywhere. You just can't help yourself, can you?'

'I run a fashion house. What do you expect?' He looked effortlessly sophisticated in a suit designed to accentuate his physique and dark good looks. 'Is that jealousy I hear in your voice?'

'Don't be ridiculous. I couldn't care less whose picture you have on your wall or who you kiss.'

'Really? Isn't that rather a liberal attitude for someone who only recently decided I was the only man in the world for her?'

Livid by his flippant response, she glared at him. 'Right now the only thing standing between you and death is the fact that I don't want more negative headlines.'

Dark brows rose above eyes that glinted with mockery. 'So much passion so early in our relationship. Not that I'm complaining. I love a woman who isn't afraid to show emotion.'

'Damn you, Luca, are you ever serious? Do you know how hard I've worked over the past few years to get people to take me seriously? This was a fresh start and then you—you…' Her hands curled into fists and she turned away from him, hating the loss of control. Hating the attraction she felt towards him. Hating him.

'And then I—what?'

'You know what! You—you kissed me. You had your hand on my—' Just thinking of the photograph made her close her eyes in horror. 'It looked as if we'd—'

'Do you ever finish your sentences? You're like a walking crossword and I'm too lazy to fill in the blanks.'

'I'm—I'm just so mad with you.'

'Don't worry about it. I'm sure it will be good for you to express honest emotion once in a while.'

'Don't mess with me, Luca.' Furious, she stabbed her finger into his chest and then wished she hadn't because all she felt was muscle. 'Be careful. I haven't eaten carbs for three months and I'm always dangerous when I'm hungry.'

'For what it's worth, I'm mad with you too, and my diet is fine. My taste has never run to women who suppress their real selves. And now let's get to the point.' The snap of his voice raised the tension in the room several more notches. 'Why the hell did you announce that we're engaged?'

'Because, thanks to you, I was about to be fired from the job I haven't even started yet!'

That drew a frown from him. 'Why would you be fired?'

'Because the director refused to work with someone with my reputation.'

He looked bemused. 'That's crazy. So you like sex and you're not afraid to show it. What's wrong with that?'

Her cheeks burned. 'What's wrong is that I want the focus to be on my skills as an actress, not on my ability to make a fool of myself with a man.'

She'd done that before and she'd lived with the mistake ever since.

He'd left another message on her phone but this time she hadn't even opened it.

It was a relief to be in Sicily, far from California.

Far from *him*.

Luca was watching her curiously. 'So you are afraid to show it. You really need to get over that. Who you choose to kiss in your own time is no one's business but your own.'

She felt like telling him it wasn't that simple. That a kiss could be used and used again. 'I didn't choose to kiss you. You grabbed me.'

'I don't remember you struggling.' He was maddeningly cool. 'It takes two people to make a kiss look like that, *tesoro*.'

'I never would have started it.'

'But you finished it.' His voice was low and threaded through with a sensuality she found off-the-scale disturbing. 'Don't be too hard on yourself. It was an understandable slip.'

'You're so full of—'

'Now, now, Miss Carmichael—' he placed his fingers over her lips '—you don't want to give the press another quote, do you? I'm sure they have a lens trained at this office even as you shriek.'

'You're finding this funny. I don't even know why you did it—why did you do it? Why the hell did you kiss me?'

He gave a careless shrug. 'You were there.'

'That's all it takes for you to kiss a woman? She just has to be there?'

'Unlike you, I don't try and deny my true nature.'

'Nice to know you're discriminating.'

'Have you played Katerina?' One dark eyebrow lifted. *Taming of the Shrew?* Because you'd be a natural. Do I need to remind you that you kissed me back?'

'I was stressed out. I hadn't eaten for two days.'

He smiled. 'So that was why you were so hungry for me.'

'Don't flatter yourself.'

'Why not? A moment ago you were telling the world you intend to spend the rest of your life with me.'

'I didn't know what else to say.' Taylor paced over to the window of his office, her heels tapping on the floor. 'I don't need all the adverse publicity right now. It was a spur of the moment thing. I didn't even think people would believe me, but they did. Apparently people are captivated by the thought of us together.'

'Of course they are. I'm the man who has publicly said on numerous occasions that he never intends to settle down and you're the wild child with a bad attitude. It's a match made in hell. How can the public not be fascinated? If you'd kept quiet the story would have died by tomorrow. As it is, you've ensured it's kept alive.'

'Stories don't die.' The words tumbled out of her mouth along with years of anxiety and pressure. 'They never die. Sometimes they lie dormant and that's even worse because you have no idea when they're going to explode in your face.'

He stared at her in bemusement. 'I have no idea what the hell you are talking about.'

Of course he didn't. And she had no intention of enlightening him. 'This is all your fault.'

'You kissed me back.'

'I wasn't talking about that, I was talking about the fact that you treated that woman badly and she sold her story to the press! If you were more sensitive, this wouldn't have happened.'

'You kissed me back.' His voice was dangerously soft and suddenly her mouth was dry and her heart was thundering.

'Or if you'd just paid her—'

'You kissed me back.'

'Yes, all right, I kissed you back!' Her head full of images she didn't want to see, her voice rose. 'But I wasn't thinking at the time.'

'I know. You were stripped down to the most basic version of yourself. The real you. I like that version much better, by the way.'

'Well, I don't,' Taylor snapped. 'I've left that version behind.'

'You might want to look in the maze. I'm sure I had my hands on that version yesterday.'

And that version of her wanted to grab him and haul his mouth back against hers. That version wanted to rip at his clothes and explore those parts of his body she hadn't already explored. That version was burning up with sexual awareness and a need so strong it took her breath away.

That version was driving her mad and had to be buried.

Just to be sure she couldn't be tempted to follow her instincts, she kept her hands locked behind her back. 'This is a joke to you, isn't it?'

'Surprisingly enough, no. There is nothing amusing about marriage or anything that goes with it.' The phone on his desk rang and then immediately stopped as his PA intercepted it from her office. 'That is about the seventieth call I've had from journalists on my private line since you so kindly announced our engagement a few hours ago. It's not working out for me. It's time we broke it off.'

'No!' Anger turned to desperation. Trying to ignore the chemistry, Taylor lifted her fingers to her temple and forced herself to breathe. 'Please. You have no idea how badly I want this job.'

His gaze was cool and unsympathetic. 'Buy cheaper shoes or, better still, wear one of the thousands of pairs you already own.'

She lowered her hand slowly. 'You think this is about shoes? About money?'

'What is it about then?'

It was about acting, but it didn't occur to anyone that she loved her job. They thought it was all about the publicity and that was her mother's fault. She'd made a name for herself as the pushiest parent in Hollywood and Taylor's reputation had suffered as a result.

Not just her reputation.

Her decision making.

'I want to be taken seriously as an actress, that's all you need to know.' She'd learned the hard way to guard the private side of her life and she did it with the tenacity of a warrior. 'I need this job to go well.'

'And for that I'm expected to marry you?'

'No, not marry me. But I thought maybe we could keep the whole engagement pretence up, just until filming is finished.'

'You thought wrong. So far we've been engaged for about

ten minutes and that's ten minutes too long as far as I'm concerned.'

The thought of having to walk out there and admit that she'd fabricated the engagement pushed her close to the edge of panic. 'You travel a lot,' she said desperately, 'we wouldn't need to see each other much. Just the odd photograph of us looking happy together would do it.'

'It wouldn't do it for me. I have no desire to tie myself to one woman, fictitious or not. It would cramp my style.' He glanced at the expensive watch on his wrist. 'I'm late to a board meeting. When I come out of that meeting I'll be behaving like a single guy so unless you want the next headlines to say I'm cheating on you, I suggest you break the news to them fast.'

'I just told them we were engaged.'

'Your problem, not mine. Tell them you came to my office and found me with another woman. Tell them anything you like—unlike you I have no problem having the real me presented to the world. But by the time I come out of my meeting I want calls asking me for a comment on how I feel about being dumped and if that doesn't happen then I'll be making a statement about dumping you. Your choice, *dolcezza*.'

With that he strode out of the room and left her standing there.

Women.

Unsettled by the depth of the chemistry and even more upset by overexposure to the word *engaged*, Luca strode towards the boardroom like a man trying to escape the hangman's noose.

He genuinely couldn't understand why anyone would choose to get married. The thought of committing to one woman for the rest of his life made him break out in a rash. Where was the pleasure in tying yourself to one woman? He could cope with female insecurity for the duration of a photo shoot, or even a single night of passion—providing it wasn't the whole night—but the thought of a lifetime of ego stroking made him contemplate entering a monastery. Or maybe not a monastery, he mused as he was momentarily distracted by the chairman's pretty executive assistant, but certainly a place where marriage was banned.

She blushed prettily. 'The board is waiting for you, Luca.'

Boring old fossils, Luca thought, suppressing a yawn. They needed blasting into the twenty-first century and he was perfectly happy to be the one to do it if only they'd let him but there was no chance of that.

As he entered the room, he estimated that the meeting would take four minutes. One minute for them to stare at him gravely and comment on how his appalling behaviour left a stain on the Corretti name and the company as a whole, another minute while they told him he wasn't going to have a seat on the main board and a further two minutes while he gave them an uncensored, unvarnished account of what he thought of them. That part promised to be entertaining.

Prepared to make full use of his two minutes, it threw him to see the chairman rise to his feet, tears in his eyes.

Tears?

Luca executed a perfect emergency stop. He was used to women crying over him, but men crying over him? That was taking things a step too far.

'Luca…' Hands outstretched, the man who had been a close friend of his grandfather's walked round the table towards him.

Preferring all physical contact to come from the opposite sex, Luca backed away hastily, crashing into a chair in the process. 'No need for the drama. I'm the sort of guy who prefers the truth without embellishment.'

'I'm not going to lie to you, we didn't see this coming.'

'Didn't see what coming?'

'Your engagement.'

The word felt as if someone was rubbing sandpaper over raw skin. 'Ah, yes. About that—'

Bursting into a stream of Italian, the man hugged him and Luca stood rigid in that embrace, thinking that if becoming engaged triggered so much uncontrollable emotion in people then he was doubly relieved he'd chosen never to do it. 'Look, there's something I need to—'

'It changes everything.'

'Marriage? Yes, I know, that's why I've never—' Luca broke off, horrified as the older man took his face in his hands.

'If you're responsible enough to take that step then you're responsible enough to have a seat at this table.'

'Scusi?'

'We're voting you in as Matteo's successor at least until the fuss dies down and he returns. Angelo thinks he can just walk in here and take over our hotel—we'll show him a united front. You're a family man, now. A true, loyal Corretti.'

Biting back the observation that the words *loyal* and *Corretti* went together about as well as *lion* and *baby gazelle*, Luca extracted himself carefully from the man's grip, thanking his lucky stars that he hadn't actually been kissed. 'So what you're telling me,' he said slowly, 'is that my track record with the House of Corretti meant nothing to you but now that I'm engaged, I'm suddenly fit to run the hotel group?'

'Running a hotel group takes more than brain power.' One of the other directors spoke up. 'It takes dedication. You have to demonstrate responsibility not just to your employees, but to your shareholders. We saw no evidence of that in your life, but it seems we were wrong. Not only that, but you've proved yourself capable of discretion. You and Taylor Carmichael are both high-profile people and yet somehow and we can't imagine how—' he beamed approvingly '—you have managed to keep this relationship a secret until now. Frankly, this has come as a shock to us, Luca.'

'It came as a shock to me too,' Luca confessed with perfect honesty. 'I didn't see it coming.'

'So what are your plans?'

Plans? He'd planned to kill the engagement rumours and move on with his life, unrestricted, but now he was rethinking fast. Being engaged seemed to have afforded him a status within the board that impressive profits and innovative thinking had failed to produce.

If that was what it took to prove to this bunch of dinosaurs that he could add value to their company, then maybe it was worth considering.

He tested the water. 'The wedding itself isn't going to happen for a while.'

That statement was met by more beams of approval.

Encouraged, Luca elaborated. 'And right now we're both so busy we're not managing to see much of each other.'

Approval turned to sympathy and Luca decided that maybe he could be the first engaged man on the planet who never actually saw his 'fiancée.' Pondering on that thought, he decided that the situation could actually be turned to his advantage. All he had to do in return for the responsibility he wanted was resist the urge to throw himself under the wheels of a passing car every time someone said the word *engaged*.

As his mind gradually emerged from the vice-like panic that came from thinking about weddings, he realised that Taylor Carmichael was probably already announcing to the world that she'd dumped him.

Knowing he had to act quickly, Luca spread his hands and smiled at the board. 'I just came here today to share the happy news, but I'm afraid I can't stay. Gutted though I am not to spend more time with you, I'm sure you understand. It's Taylor's first day of filming down at the docklands and I want to just go over there and be supportive, because—because—' never having been supportive before, he floundered for a plausible reason for his actions '—because that's what engaged people do.' Truthfully he had absolutely no idea what engaged people did. All he knew was that he had nothing in common with them. 'I want to be there for her.'

Fortunately the board seemed impressed. 'Of course. After Matteo's behaviour at the wedding that demonstration of loyalty is just what the public need to see. Who would have thought you would be the one to add sobriety to the Corretti family name.'

Sobriety?

Luca recoiled in alarm. He was prepared to live behind a facade of respectability just to prove to these old codgers that he could do more for the company than a whole boardroom full of men in suits, but being accused of sobriety made him wonder if it was worth it.

'Go.' Visibly moved, the chairman waved his hand towards the door. 'We'll have a meeting of the hotel executive committee tomorrow evening and we look forward to hearing your ideas for boosting the hotel business then. Bring your fiancée!'

Biting back the comment that his ideas would have been the same whether he were engaged or not, Luca left the room not sure if he were in the frying pan or the fire.

Whichever, there was no doubt in his mind that he needed to get to the docklands where filming was taking place before Taylor ruined everything. He'd tell her he was willing to go along with this whole engagement thing just as long as it got him a seat on the main board.

How hard could it be?

CHAPTER FOUR

'WHEN ARE YOU getting married?'

'Tell us how you met Luca Corretti.'

'Why didn't you attend the wedding together?'

Journalists pressed around her, trapping her with a volley of questions until Taylor wanted to scream at them to leave her alone but she couldn't react because there, at the edge of the pack, watching her with a warning in his eyes was Santo Corretti.

He hadn't said a word but she'd got the message.

If she didn't handle this well, she was off the film.

He wouldn't save her.

And how could she handle it well? Thanks to Luca's refusal to play along with her, there was nothing to handle. As soon as she told them there was no engagement, it would be over.

The day was turning into a bad dream.

She'd already ordered herself a taxi and in the meantime she was stalling, waiting for it to arrive. Once she told them the truth she'd be on her own. She had no illusions about that. She needed an escape route.

And once she was safely away from here, she'd rethink her life. She didn't have much choice, did she? Her past was a constant roadblock to her dream of being taken seriously as an actress. Maybe she should give up on film and work in theatre instead. Maybe she could fly to England and base herself there. They had Stratford on Avon and The Globe.

Swallowing down the lump in her throat, she told herself that the first thing she was going to do when she was safely away from here was eat something. The second was to give that Portia woman Luca's home address and all his personal details. They deserved each other.

The loud roar of an engine made heads turn.

Taylor's heart beat faster. So this was it. 'I have something to tell you—'

But the journalists weren't looking at her. They were staring at a red Ferrari hurtling towards them at a terrifying speed.

At any other time the car would have made her drool, but right now the only car she was interested in was her taxi and this definitely wasn't it.

She felt a flash of panic. Already some of the journalists were turning back to her, waiting for her to finish her sentence. It was too late to back down. She was going to have to go ahead and tell them the truth about Luca. Santo Corretti would be so disgusted he'd leave her to it. She was going to have to elbow her way out of this mob alone and just hope the taxi showed up before she was ripped to pieces.

The sports car showed no sign of slowing and she saw several journalists mutter to one another in alarm before taking a few precautionary steps backwards.

Just when it appeared the driver was going to mow them down he hit the brakes, sending a cloud of dust rising upwards. And Taylor simply stared because there, seated behind the wheel, his eyes hidden by a pair of dark glasses that made him look insanely attractive, was Luca Corretti.

A female journalist standing nearby reached into her bag for lipgloss and Taylor felt the anger start to boil inside her.

This was all his fault.

Not only had he created this whole situation with his careless lack of concern for other people, but he'd refused to go along with her plan to bail them both out. And now he had the nerve to turn up here to make sure she'd confessed to her crime in public.

Her anger grew as he vaulted from the car and strolled towards the journalists with indolent grace. 'So maybe I broke the speed limit just a little bit—' playing to the crowd, he gave a wicked smile that held no trace of regret or apology '—but some things are worth rushing for and a beautiful woman is one of those.'

Furious that he could be so relaxed when her life was in shreds, Taylor elbowed her way through the journalists, who retreated in fascination, their professional sensors telling them that they were about to witness something worth writing about.

Taylor didn't care. She was off the film anyway. How much worse could it get?

'Luca Corretti, you are the most—'

His hands cupped her face and his mouth covered hers. His kiss was hot, explicit and devastating, and when he finally lifted his dark head enough for her to speak, the only sound she was capable of was a moan. Because there was no way she was moaning in public, she stayed silent.

'Sorry, *tesoro*, you were saying?' Slumberous dark eyes looked down at her. 'You wanted to tell me that you missed me, no? That I am the sexiest man in the world? The most clever? The most amusing?' Sliding his arm around her shoulders, he turned to face the journalists, his smile disarming. 'She is struck dumb.'

A ripple of laughter spread across the crowd.

Taylor was so shaken by that kiss, she couldn't focus. All she wanted to do was lock her hands in that glossy dark hair, pull his head down to her and kiss him again. And again—

'Luca—'

'*Mi dispiace...*' Turning towards her, he leaned his forehead against hers and smiled that smile that made women forget how to put one leg in front of the other to walk away. 'Forgive me for not making it here on time. I am a rat. A total bastard. I don't deserve you.'

She stared at him, eyes locked with his, hypnotised by the sheer power of the chemistry. It wrapped itself around her like metal bands, holding her trapped.

A sea of excited questions washed up against the wall of their own private sexual cocoon.

'So it really is true?' A female journalist thrust a microphone towards them. 'Luca, you always said you weren't the marrying kind. What's changed?'

Taylor wanted to ask the same question. 'Yes,' she muttered through clenched teeth, 'do tell us what changed.' But relief spread through her, taking with it her anger.

He was going to play along. For now, she was safe and that was all that mattered. They could work out the detail later.

His fingers stroked her face gently. 'I realised there is nothing I want more than to be engaged to Taylor.'

Another journalist stepped closer. 'You've just broken a million women's hearts.'

'I'm only interested in one woman's heart.' He leaned closer to her, his mouth by her ear. 'How long am I supposed to keep this up?'

She went from wanting to punch him to wanting to laugh out loud and not just because she was relieved he'd decided to go along with her plan. She stood on tiptoe and brushed her lips along the dark shadow of his jaw. 'Mess this up and I'll sentence you to death by a thousand Portias.'

'Portia?' His tone was innocent. 'I've never met anyone called Portia.'

To the watching journalists it looked like a romantic exchange and she heard someone sigh wistfully.

'All right, that's enough romance for one day,' Luca murmured under his breath, easing away from her and address-

ing the crowd. 'All this attention is very distracting for my…
fiancée.'

Taylor wondered if she was the only one who noticed he
stumbled over the word. 'Yes. I need to get on with my job.
So if there are no more questions—'

'Tell us about the proposal. And why aren't you wearing
a ring?'

Taylor froze. Deprived of sleep, her brain failed to think
of a response but Luca pushed his hand into his pocket and
there, dangling from his fingers and sparkling in the Sicilian
sunshine, was a huge diamond ring.

'I chose an extra big one,' he drawled, 'to hold her in place
so she can't run away when I misbehave. And also so that
when she's angry with me she can throw it and knock me unconscious. I've been keeping it with me because we hadn't
exactly planned to go public with this today.'

Wondering where he'd managed to find such an incredible
ring at such short notice, Taylor allowed him to slip it onto
the appropriate finger and smiled her most romantic smile
while the female journalists gazed on with envy and greed.

'Taylor, can you tell me in a single word how you felt when
he gave you that ring?'

That was easy enough. 'It was a moment beyond words.
I was speechless.'

'And that was the best possible response because speechless is how I prefer my women.' At his most shocking, Luca
kept her hand tightly in his and ploughed his way through the
flock of press back to his Ferrari. 'And now if you'll excuse
us, we are going to seek some privacy to do, er, to do those
things engaged people do. Santo, when you find a director
with balls, call us.'

She was still on the film.

Weak with relief, Taylor closed her eyes, leaned her head
against the passenger seat and let the wind blow through her

hair. Beneath her she felt the power of the engine and smiled. The car was a glorious, sinful expression of luxury and speed and part of her just wanted to push him aside, grab the wheel and slam her foot to the floor. She wanted to swing round tight hairpin bends and drive the car to the edge in every sense of the word.

But Taylor Carmichael didn't do things like that.

Not any more.

Taylor Carmichael behaved herself at all times.

Taylor Carmichael was never, ever going to be caught out again.

She opened her eyes feeling light-headed. Somehow, she was still on the film. Unfortunately she was also with Luca Corretti, a man as capable of extinguishing her good fortune as he was at nurturing it. 'Where are we going?'

'Somewhere away from all those people who seem determined to share in our special, private moment.' He shifted gears smoothly. The engine roared and they overtook car after car as they sped along the coast road.

Taylor, who normally hated being driven, wondered why she didn't feel nervous. 'So why the change of heart? I thought you didn't want to be engaged.'

'I don't. But I don't mind pretending to be engaged for as long as it suits me. I gained instant respectability. The board cried over my instant transformation.'

'They cried? Really?' The wind whipped her hair around her face and she anchored it with her hand, exhilarated by the speed, a smile on her lips. 'That's almost funny.'

'I agree.' Leaning on his horn as he executed a death-defying acceleration to pass another car, he threw her a slanting smile that made her think of nothing but sex. 'Who would have thought it? We appear to share a sense of humour. And a love of speed.'

Unsettled at the thought of having anything in common

with him, Taylor frowned. 'We'll be sharing an ambulance if you don't slow down.'

'Oh, come on—' his eyes were back on the road '—you're a woman who was built to go fast.'

'I hate driving fast.'

'No, you don't. You love it.'

'You're reckless.' She told herself it was the speed of the car not the wicked curve of his mouth that made her heart beat a little bit faster.

'Has it ever occurred to you that it's the other drivers who are going too slowly? There should be a sign—Dithering Is Dangerous. And you should know that fast is my default speed for everything except sex.'

'I don't need to know that.' She'd been trying not to think about sex but it was impossible around this man. Everything about him screamed masculinity, even the way he handled the car. She looked away quickly, trying to forget the sheer animal passion they'd unleashed together. And that had been just a single kiss. Her brief moment of relief turned to dread as she realised that her desperate, impulsive attempt to protect her position on the film had placed her in a position where she was going to have to spend time with this man. This man who tempted her more than any other. Despite the baking sun her skin felt suddenly cold. 'I already know enough and I think you are the most infuriating man I've ever met.'

'No, you don't.' His voice was a soft, masculine purr. 'I make you laugh and we understand each other, *dolcezza*, because we are so alike.'

It felt as if someone were squeezing her throat. 'I'm nothing like you. And you drive me mad.'

'You just think that because you're hungry. A hungry woman is always irritable. When did you last eat?'

'Eat? I don't want to eat.' She just wanted to get out of the car. She wanted to wind the clock back and find another way of extracting herself from this mess.

She didn't do this. She didn't put herself in the way of temptation.

'Of course you want to eat. You're permanently starving but for some reason you suppress every appetite you ever experience.' Without warning, he took a right turn, roared into a small village and cut the engine, oblivious to the stares he earned from the locals. 'Wait here.'

He disappeared for a few moments and then reappeared and dropped a bag onto her lap. 'Never let it be said I don't know what a woman really wants.'

The smell made her stomach rumble and Taylor opened the bag curiously. 'A cheeseburger? You think that's what a woman really wants?'

He leaned towards her and for a terrifying, breathless moment she thought he was going to kiss her again but he simply smiled that maddening smile that made her stomach curl. 'I'm good at understanding a woman's hidden desires, *dolcezza*.'

Pride kept her still in her seat. 'Evidently not, because I have no desire for a cheeseburger.' Her stomach growled loudly and his smile widened as he pulled back from her and started the engine.

'I'll leave you to argue with your stomach about that one. But while you're engaged to me, you'll eat carbs. Otherwise one of us will kill the other and that is not going to produce the headlines you're hoping for.' Eyes in the mirror, he executed a perfect U-turn and rejoined the main highway while Taylor stared at the cheeseburger, remembering the time she'd sneaked out with friends for a burger and been caught by her mother. She'd been twelve years old, excited by her first-ever invitation to join a group of girls and feeling almost normal for the first time in her life, when her mother had come storming into the restaurant and dragged it out of her hand, demanding to know why she was so determined to ruin her career.

Taylor closed the bag and gripped the top so that she wasn't tempted, but the smell wouldn't leave her alone.

Her mouth watered. Her stomach mewed.

She made an impatient sound. The day was turning from a bad dream into a nightmare. 'You're cruel, you know that, don't you?'

'Just eat it and spare me the drama.'

'I can't.' Her fingers tightened on the bag. 'It's on the forbidden list.'

'Scusi?'

'The forbidden list. The list of things I can't do.'

'You're seriously telling me you have a list of things you can't do?'

'I don't expect you to understand,' Taylor snapped, 'but I can't eat this. For a start my character in the movie is supposed to be slender.'

'Your character will be found strangled by her infuriated fiancée if you don't eat something substantial soon.' He pulled back onto the coast road. 'Tell me more about this forbidden list. I think I might have one too.'

'You? You have to be kidding.'

'Well, I have a list—the difference is that mine is called my priority list. What else is on yours?'

Spending time with men like him.

'Everything that is bad for me and will wreck my career.'

'So it's also called the boring list. I suggest you flip that list and do everything on it, starting with eating food that's bad for you and tastes good. Open that bag and feed the real you. Go on. You know you want to.'

She did want to. She wanted to so badly.

Oh, hell, why not?

Tired and starving hungry, Taylor gave in to temptation. It wasn't as if one hamburger was going to kill her.

Trying to block out the sound of her mother saying 'think of your career' she closed her eyes and took a bite. Flavour exploded in her mouth. She moaned. 'I think that might be the best thing I've ever tasted. Find a bin, quickly. I have to throw it away before I'm tempted to take another bite.'

'Take another bite. And then another. When your stomach is full and you're not behaving like a she-wolf stalking her prey, we'll talk.'

Flavour slicing through her willpower, Taylor took another bite. 'OK, you win. When filming is over I'm going to buy a truckload of these. How do I ask for it in Italian?'

'You ask for *pane con la milza*.'

'*Pane con la milza*. That's Italian for cheeseburger?' She took another mouthful and chewed slowly, savouring every moment. 'I know that *pane* means "bread," and *con* means "with." So *milza* must be—what? Beef? Ham?'

'Spleen.'

Taylor stopped chewing. 'Pardon?'

'*Milza* means "spleen."'

At the point of swallowing, she choked. 'I'm eating a spleen burger? You fed me spleen burger?'

'Your translation is less than elegant but yes, the meat is spleen. *Pane con la milza* is a delicacy, particularly around Palermo. My grandmother used to make it in her kitchen when I was a little boy.'

She dropped the rest of the 'burger' in the bag and put it on the floor of his car. 'Pull over. Now.'

'Why?'

'I'm going to throw up.'

'Throw up in my Ferrari and this engagement is off. Nothing is worth that. *Cristo*, Taylor, stop behaving like a wimpy female.' He flung her an impatient look before fixing his eyes on the road again. 'What is that phrase you use? Put your big-girl pants on. But not literally—I prefer you in something more revealing. A thong works for me. Does that phrase exist? Put your sexy-girl thong on? Whatever—show some guts.'

'Thanks to you I just ate guts.'

'And even as we speak the nutrition will be flowing into your starved veins. Your starved body should be thanking me.'

'You have a problem with my body? That's odd because it certainly didn't seem that way when you were ripping my clothes off a few days ago.' She had the satisfaction of seeing his hands tighten on the wheel.

'I didn't see enough of it to judge.'

The atmosphere in the car had shifted dangerously and she wished she'd kept the conversation on the topic of food. Wiping her fingers on a napkin, she shuddered. 'Do not ever mention this particular meal again. I do not want to even think about the fact I just ate a—never mind.'

'I never would have thought you were squeamish. Meat is meat.'

'I don't often eat meat and when I do I like to know what I'm eating before I eat it. Now I understand why all your relationships have been short. I don't think I can even *pretend* to love you enough to marry you. You drive me crazy.'

'Anyone choosing to get married has to be crazy, so I don't see that as a problem.' He slowed the car, waiting as a pair of electric gates opened slowly, and then accelerated along a drive bordered by tall cypress trees.

'Where are we?' She threw a glance at his profile, wondering why he was so firmly against marriage. She decided it was probably because he lived his life surrounded by gorgeous women.

'We're somewhere exclusive where we can be assured of privacy.' The tyres crunched over gravel as he pulled up outside a beautiful building built from honey-coloured stone.

A woman appeared from nowhere. 'Luca!' She burst into a stream of fluent Italian and Luca replied in the same language. Taylor glanced around her, trying to ignore the fact that hearing him speak in that beautiful, lilting language made her tummy tighten.

SARAH MORGAN   67

Impatient with herself, she reminded herself that any time her self-control weakened around him she just needed to think of him feeding her a spleen burger. Most of all she needed to remember that there was nothing romantic about this situation.

Which suited her just fine.

Never again was she trusting a man. Or any other person for that matter. She was using Luca Corretti, just as he was using her.

Having reminded herself of that, it was doubly unsettling when the woman walked across to her and took her hands, her eyes filling.

Taylor suppressed her natural impulse to back away. 'Er, *bueno*, er...' She glanced hopelessly at Luca, who rolled his eyes.

'That's Spanish. What are you trying to say?'

Taylor felt her face turn scarlet with embarrassment. 'I'm trying to be friendly and say hello.'

'If it's after midday you can just say *buona sera*. This is Geovana. She speaks some English, although she might not be familiar with "spleen burger."'

'You have no idea how relieved I am to hear that.'

Geovana's hands tightened on hers. 'Welcome.'

Touched by the warmth shown to her, Taylor looked at Luca. 'How do I say "I'm pleased to be here" in Italian?'

'I amarlo così tanto la sua folle.'

She repeated it slowly and was stunned when Geovana flung her arms round her and hugged her tightly. Unused to being hugged, Taylor held herself rigid. 'Oh! This is...nice and...welcoming.' Most of all it was unfamiliar. She frowned slightly, feeling something inside her unravel. Geovana was warm and plump and...motherly. Taylor swallowed. Her own mother had seen her as a meal ticket, as a means to live out her own dreams, not as a daughter to be hugged. Their conversations had only ever been about how Taylor could do more, be more, never about who she was or what she wanted, and it had never, ever been about affection. They'd parted ways when Taylor was seventeen and hadn't spoken since.

When Geovana finally released her only to kiss her on both cheeks, Taylor felt confused, raw and vulnerable.

'She likes you,' Luca said in a flat drawl, 'that's a compliment. Come on, I'll show you to our bedroom suite.'

Our bedroom? She decided to ignore that until they were alone. 'Doesn't she usually like your girlfriends?'

'She's never met any of them.' Taking her hand, Luca strode into the house as if he owned it, crossed the beautiful, light-filled entrance hall and up a curved staircase.

'Why hasn't she met any of them?' Taylor tugged at her hand but he didn't release her. His fingers were cool and strong. 'I assumed this hotel is one of your regular sex hideouts. Or do you smuggle your women in and out through the window?' She tugged at her hand, harder this time, and this time he released her.

Relief flowed through her and she promised herself that from now on she'd keep a physical distance from him. No touching. She had enough problems without adding to them.

'This isn't a hotel.' He pushed open a door and walked into a room that took her breath away. Through the open French doors the view stretched across a garden to a vineyard and, beyond that, in the distance, the towering peak of Mount Etna.

Taylor decided she'd never seen a more perfect view in her life. 'Wow. You have an eye for beauty, I'll give you that. It's stunning. And so private.' Reluctantly, she dragged her eyes from the view to look at him. 'If this isn't a hotel, then what is it?'

'It's my home.' He shrugged off his jacket and removed his tie. 'And I don't bring women here, so don't get too comfortable. Strictly speaking I should have blindfolded you before I brought you to my private lair.'

'Why don't you bring women here?'

'Because my home is a place to relax and women are exhausting.' He strolled across the sunlit room and placed his cufflinks in a dish on the nightstand, 'From their uncanny ability to misinterpret everything a man says or does, to their endless demands for reassurance, including such well-loved phrases as "Does this dress make me look fat?" and—every man's favourite—"What are you thinking?"'

'Yeah, that must be a tough one for a guy like you who never bothers thinking. If you had bothered to think you wouldn't have messed up so badly with Portia.' She used sarcasm to cover up the way he made her feel. It wasn't just the sexual chemistry that terrified her, it was the buzz she had from talking to him.

'I didn't mess up with Portia. That relationship ended precisely when I intended it to. I consider that to be a success.'

'But if you'd ended it more thoughtfully we wouldn't be in this position.'

'In what position? Suddenly we're both respectable. It's a miracle.' With a complete lack of self-consciousness he undid the rest of the buttons of his shirt, allowing it to fall open. His trousers rode low on his lean hips, revealing toned, male abs, and Taylor averted her eyes, ignoring the dangerous curl of warmth that spread through her body.

'Thanks, but I can live without the striptease.'

'Is it bothering you?'

Exasperation mingled with a much more dangerous emotion. 'No, it isn't bothering me. But I'm the sort of person who needs personal space. We should have stayed at my hotel.' The glimpse had been brief, but the image of his bronzed, fit body was seared onto her brain. 'I have a suite with two rooms.'

'I can't stand hotels.'

'And yet you want to run the family business?'

'That's different.' He shrugged, his tone bored. 'That's just about proving a point. And if we're going to be engaged then I need space too. I'm not good at being trapped with a woman.'

But now they were both trapped and he was looking at her, assessing her with that lazy, sexy stare that was so much a part of him until she felt as if her skin might catch fire.

Desperately, she steered the subject onto safer ground. 'So tell me about Geovana.' She thought about the warmth the other woman had shown her. 'Why did she hug me so tightly? When I said I was pleased to be here, she almost strangled me.'

'That's because you didn't say you were pleased to be here. You said you were so in love with me it's driving you crazy.'

She gaped at him. 'I said what you told me to say.'

'Yes. And you were remarkably fluent. Very impressive for a non-Italian speaker.'

Mouth tightening, she tapped her foot on the floor. 'I suppose you think that's really funny. Like teaching a toddler to use rude words.'

'Since I don't intend to ever marry, that's an experience I'm not going to be in a position to comment on but strangely enough I didn't do it to be funny. I did it because we're supposed to be engaged. You're not the only one who can act a part when required.'

'That's why she hugged me? Because I told her I was crazy about you?'

'So it would seem.' A ghost of a smile touched his mouth. 'Today is probably the happiest day of her life. Geovana had given up on seeing me bring a woman home.'

'Because no woman would put up with you.' But part of her wondered whether there was a deeper reason for his aversion to marriage. Her instincts told her there was more to it than simply a love of a playboy lifestyle. 'Have you known her a long time?'

'Since I was five years old.'

Taylor felt a twinge of envy at the warmth of his relationship with the woman.

She didn't have anyone in her life she was close to. No one

she could trust as Luca clearly trusted Geovana. It was obvious that the older woman adored him.

'How did you meet her?' She asked the question as they walked up the stairs towards the bedroom.

'She was our nanny until my mother fired her in a fit of jealousy.'

'You had a nanny?' She bit her tongue. Of course he'd had a nanny. He came from a rich family. He hadn't been used as the breadwinner by an ambitious mother while he was still in nappies. 'Did your mother work?'

'It was a full-time job trying to keep my father happy.'

She was about to question that statement when he started to unbuckle his belt. 'Whoa. Rewind. I do not need to see you naked. This engagement is fake, remember?'

'There is no way I'll forget that, *dolcezza*. Just make sure you don't.'

'Oh, please—there is no way I'll forget that.'

'Don't be so sure. Every woman I meet thinks she's going to be the one to change my ways and drag me to the altar.'

Turning her back on him, Taylor paced around the room, noticing the art on the walls and the beautiful stylish touches. There were no photographs. Nothing personal. 'You are known for living the high life. We are going to have to work extra hard to convince people this is real. Even pretending is giving you a hunted look. I'm going to have to teach you to act.'

'I can act. I don't need your help.'

'And I may not need yours if Santo doesn't manage to replace the director.' Battling a rush of insecurity, Taylor walked through the French doors onto the pretty balcony with its glorious views of the Sicilian countryside. 'It's gorgeous. Are you sure the press won't find us here?'

'Of course I'm not sure. They can find us anywhere, that's their job.' He seemed completely indifferent to the possibility

and she felt her own pulse rate quicken as she walked back
into the bedroom.

'Don't you care?'

'Why would I?'

'It's an invasion of privacy.'

'I've never seen the need to hide what I do.' He removed
his shirt and dropped it onto the bed. The flex of hard, honed
muscle across his wide shoulders had her staring, and because
this was the day where nothing was going her way that was
the moment he turned and caught her.

'Enjoying the view?'

'Not particularly. And I have no idea why you're undress-
ing.'

'Purely for your entertainment, *dolcezza*.' Sending her a
sexy smile, he unclipped his watch. 'And for the entertainment of any photographers who happen to have long lenses
trained on my bedroom. I'd hate to disappoint them. Oh—
and because I intend to take a shower.'

'Photographers?' Horrified, she looked from him to the
long windows that offered a view into the distance. 'Can this
house be seen from the road?'

'I have no idea. I suppose we'll find out now you're staying here.'

'I'm not staying here…' She stumbled over the words in
her panic, tripping over her bag as she backed to the door
and opened it. 'If the press could be watching, I can't stay.
I have to go somewhere I know I can't be photographed—I
have to—'

'You have to calm down.' Luca strode over to her and
pushed the door shut with the flat of his hand, saying something to her in Italian. '*Cristo*, Taylor, why all the drama?
You're not on set now.'

'I hate being photographed.'

'Yes, I'm starting to get that part. Even I'm not that ob-
tuse.' His keen gaze was fixed on her face. 'What I don't get

is why. You're an actress. You're photographed all the time. It's part of the job.'

'And I accept it when I'm out filming, or at a premiere or even when I'm out having fun because I know I can never go anywhere without being recognised any more, but I have to know I'm safe when I'm at h-home. I don't want to be photographed when I—think I'm alone.' She was stammering. 'I deserve that. Doesn't everyone deserve that?'

'Yes, I suppose so, if that's what they want. And now are you going to tell me what happened?'

Her stomach felt as if someone had tied a knot in it. 'What do you mean?'

'No one freaks out like that without a reason. So tell me the reason. What happened?'

'Nothing happened.' She had no intention of talking about it, especially not to him. She'd learned the hard way that no one could be trusted. Thinking back to how naive she'd been at seventeen made her want to curl up in embarrassment but at least she'd learned the lesson. 'I'm a private person, that's all. There's nothing wrong with that.'

'Except that, like most celebrities, the press considers you public property.'

His choice of phrase triggered something inside her. 'I'm a person, not property. I am not anyone's meal ticket!'

'Taylor—'

'Enough, OK? I don't even know why we're talking about this. I just hate the press, that's all you need to know. I don't want to stay somewhere they can see me! If they're pushing a camera in my face, I want to know about it.' Shocked to discover just how much emotion was still simmering deep inside her, Taylor reached for the door handle but his hand covered hers.

'*Cristo*, you're shaking.'

'No, I'm not.'

'You are the most confusing woman I've ever met,' he breathed. 'Ballsy one minute and fragile the next.'

'I'm not fragile.'

There was a long pause. 'I'll brief my security team. I'll make sure this place is like a fortress. The only photographs those bastards get will be the ones we want them to take. Us doing engagement stuff—whatever that is. Talking of which, we'd better find out what we're supposed to do.' He released her and strolled across the bedroom as if nothing had happened, leaving Taylor shaken. It unsettled her to know she was nowhere near as in control as she liked to think she was.

Pulling herself together, she looked at him. 'What are you doing now?'

He keyed something into his phone. 'Given that you and I are clueless, I'm doing a search for the typical behaviour of engaged people. There has to be a website. It's probably called getmeoutofhere.com. Or possibly killmenow.org.' The remark was typical of him and for some reason that normality helped relax her.

'We're not just engaged, we're newly engaged.'

'And the significance of that is…?'

'The first glow of excitement has yet to wear off. We have to be supersickly.'

'No worries. The thought of being engaged makes me feel more sickly than you can possibly imagine.'

'And you fed me spleen burger. Need I say more?'

'No, but you're a woman so no doubt you will anyway. If you want to sit down, sit on the bed. It can't be seen from the window unless they have a lens shaped like a periscope.' It was the only reference he made to her sudden loss of control. 'Here you are. Ten habits of engaged couples. Can you believe someone researched that and then wrote about it? What a total waste of a life.'

Taylor glanced from the window to the bed and decided to

follow his advice. She slid off her shoes and sat cross-legged on the end of the bed. 'Go on. Read it out.'

He was staring at her legs. 'What are you doing?'

'Relaxing. I do yoga. It's good for the core and helps keep me flexible.'

'Flexible?' His voice slightly rough, Luca lifted his gaze from her legs to her face, his phone forgotten. 'How flexible?'

The temperature in the room shot up and suddenly all she could think of was the way his mouth had felt on hers.

'Flexible enough to make sure that when we're seen in public you're looking very tired.' Unable to resist teasing him, she wrapped one leg behind her neck and his brows rose.

'That position has amazing possibilities but there's no way I'd look tired in public. I have endless stamina. Maybe you'll be the one who is looking tired, *tesoro*, from my male demands.'

Her heart thudded a little harder. 'I've been working with a trainer for months in preparation for this role. I can cope with any physical demands you care to throw my way.'

'Is that a challenge?'

'Absolutely not.' Taylor swallowed and allowed her leg to slide back into its original position. 'So what advice does your website offer?'

His eyes lingered on hers and then eventually he looked back at the screen. 'Touching.'

'Pardon?'

'According to this, newly engaged couples touch all the time. They can't bear to be next to each other and not feel each other. Does that mean I have permission to stroke your breasts in public? Maybe this won't be so bad after all.'

'Public. Of course. We have to be seen in public.' Taylor pushed away thoughts of his hands on her breasts. 'We need to be seen, otherwise no one is going to believe this is real. We should go out for dinner or something.'

'What's the point of that? You don't eat anything.'

'All the better. People will assume my love for you is putting me off my food.'

'Just as long as you don't expect me to be off my food too, because I have no intention of starving myself for the role.' He scanned the screen, his expression comical. '*Cristo*, is there anything good about being engaged?'

'Why ask me? I've never been engaged before either. Nor do I want to be.'

'No?' His gaze lifted to hers. 'Then that makes us a perfect pair. So what happened to you to put you off relationships?'

Her heart thudded a little bit faster. 'Life.'

'You mean a man.'

Would a real man take advantage of a vulnerable girl? Would a real man cynically manipulate someone's feelings for his own benefit? She felt the panic stir deep inside her and squashed it down. 'Well, he had a penis, if that's what you mean. But apart from that no, I wouldn't call him a man.' The words tasted like acid in her mouth and they must have sounded the same way because he lowered his phone, his dark gaze suddenly sharp.

'Is this guy the reason you hate the press? What did he do?'

Why on earth had she started this conversation? Especially with a man as shallow and superficial as Luca Corretti. She was surprised he'd even asked the question. What did he know about loneliness? Or vulnerability, come to that. He came from a huge family. He had no idea what it was like to have no one. He would never in a million years understand what had happened to her.

'It isn't relevant.'

'I'm your fiancé. If you have something in your past that had that big an impact on you, I need to know about it.'

'No, you don't.' She felt the panic rise from deep inside her and block her throat. 'My past is none of your business.'

'For someone who claims this is in the "past" you look pretty stressed out.'

'It's being with you that makes me stressed out. And what about you?' She turned it back on him. 'Anything in your past I need to know about?'

'Nothing at all.' He deflected her question with ease. 'My life is an open book.'

No one's life was an open book, she knew that now. There were hidden corners, areas of darkness, a graveyard of secrets.

She wondered what his were.

While she was musing on the comment he'd made about his mother, he strode across the room, picked up the phone and spoke in Italian. 'I'm taking you out to dinner. My team will book us a table at Da Giovanni. It's very elegant. And high-profile. You can push a lettuce leaf around your plate and gaze at me adoringly.'

'You'll have to gaze at me adoringly too.'

'I can do that as long as you don't get confused and start thinking it's real.'

'When I grab a gun and shoot myself through the head you'll know I'm starting to think our relationship is real,' she told him in a cool tone. 'Until then, you're safe. Unfortunately I don't have any faith that you are capable of even acting the part of a man in love, so concentrate because I'm going to give you some hints.'

'I've already told you I don't need an acting lesson.'

She ignored that. 'The best way to convincingly play emotion is to conjure up the feeling. So if I'm playing someone sad, I try and remember a time when I was sad.'

'I've never been engaged so I can't conjure up the horror that went with it.'

'Very funny, but not helpful. Tonight you have to look as if I'm the only woman in the world for you. Is there any chance you can do that?'

'Are all the other women in the world dead? I suppose if that were the case, I might be relieved to be shackled to you. You're not bad once you're fed.'

Taylor clenched her jaw. 'This is a nightmare. You are never going to be able to act as if you're engaged. It isn't in your nature.'

'Watch me prove you wrong. I can act. I can dredge emotions from deep inside me or wherever it is emotions are stored. You want happiness, right? I can do happiness as long as I'm not expected to associate it with relationships.'

Taylor breathed slowly. 'All right, let's try this another way. What is the happiest moment you can remember?'

He didn't hesitate. 'The day they delivered my Ferrari.'

'Fine! Tonight, you are going to look at me as if I'm your Ferrari.'

'Do I get to put your top down?'

'You are infuriating!' So why did she want to laugh? 'This was such a bad idea. You'll blow it and this will be the shortest engagement on record.'

'I am not going to blow it. I love my Ferrari. I love my Ferrari.' He muttered the words under his breath and shot her a glance. 'Perhaps I'd better dress you in red, just so that there's a similarity.'

Taylor shook her head in despair. 'And on that note, I have to go back to my hotel. I can't go out to dinner in the same clothes I've been wearing all day, and anyway, if we're going to stay here I need to pack up my things and move them here.'

'One of the advantages of being engaged to the head of a fashion house is that clothes aren't a problem.' He sent a quick message on his phone. 'If we're going to be seen together, you might as well showcase something from Corretti.'

'So now you're using me for free publicity?'

'Of course I'm using you. That's what this is all about. I'm using you. You're using me.'

Of course I'm using you.

Taylor ignored the uneasy feeling in her stomach. She told

herself this was different. Yes, she'd been used before but
Luca was right—this time she was using him too.

And that made this different from all the times people had
used her before.

CHAPTER FIVE

LUCA DREW UP in a no-parking zone in front of the pretty waterside restaurant.

'You can't park here.' Taylor turned her head, the sun glinting on her sleek, shiny hair. She'd twisted it skilfully into an elaborate confection on the back of her head and fastened it with a jewelled pin that made her look very much the movie star. 'It says no parking.'

'Do you always obey rules?' The artist in Luca admired the perfect lines of her jaw and cheekbones, those beautiful cat-like eyes and the hint of a pout on that kissable mouth. 'That dress looks good on you.'

'I know. That's why I picked it.' Her cool, confident response threw him.

Raised by a woman who had needed constant reassurance and working in an industry defined by its dedication to narcissism, he was conditioned to offer praise and reassurance. These days it fell from his lips unprompted, but Taylor appeared to have no need for his approval. Presented with a choice of dresses, she'd selected one instantly, without hesitation or consultation. The only help she'd needed from him was fastening the zip.

'Of course you'd look better out of that dress.'

'I try not to trigger horrible headlines.'

'Really? I try and trigger horrible headlines on a daily

basis. If I don't read at least one bad thing about myself every day I take a long look at my behaviour and try harder to be shocking.'

Her response to that was to roll her eyes but he could see she was holding back laughter and he hid his own smile because he didn't want her to know she made him laugh.

She held everything back, he thought, remembering the way she'd tried to resist the explosive chemistry in the maze. Always up for a challenge, he wondered how hard he'd have to push before that control cracked.

She glanced towards the restaurant. 'Isn't this place a bit obvious? I would have chosen somewhere more discreet. That would have been my normal behaviour.'

'But not mine, *dolcezza*.' He flipped her chin gently with the tip of his finger. 'You're with me and I refuse to slink around like a criminal. You're living by my list now and your idea of forbidden is my idea of compulsory. Get used to it.'

'If we're a couple then my list is as important and valid as yours.'

'Not if it contains things like "don't speed" and "never park in a no-parking zone." The idea of marriage isn't to die of boredom.' Reaching across, he unfastened her seat belt, the backs of his fingers brushing against the softness of her breasts as he released the strap. The punch of desire was so powerful he sucked in a breath at the exact moment Taylor flattened herself to the seat.

'Hey, don't push your luck.'

'We're engaged. That means my luck ran out a long time ago. And what is the point of an engagement if you can't touch? Or is it simply to leave an enormous hole in a guy's bank account and set one lucky jeweller up for early retirement?' Gripped by a flash of instantaneous lust, Luca found himself looking at her mouth and that mouth was so smooth, so feminine, it seemed like a terrible waste not to just go ahead and kiss it. Never one to deny himself, he did just that.

Fire and flame licked around the edges of his nerve endings. Within seconds he was rock hard. What had started as exploration shifted to something so primal and basic that he forgot everything except the urge to strip her naked and get his hands on her glorious body. He wanted to drive into her and watch all those restrictions she placed on herself unravel.

His tongue was in her mouth, tangling with hers, when she shoved at his chest.

'This is an engagement, not a one-night stand. You don't have to cram the entire relationship into six hours.' She was out of the car so quickly she almost stumbled and Luca stared after her for a moment, his mind temporarily wiped. She was as jumpy as a kangaroo on a trampoline and yet she was the one who had lectured him on playing his part properly. How the hell was he expected to play his part when she was running away from him? He didn't claim to be an expert on being engaged but was willing to bet sprinting in the opposite direction during a kiss counted as less than convincing behaviour.

He chose to ignore the tiny part of his brain that was telling him the kiss had nothing to do with role play.

Infuriated that she wasn't putting more effort into it, he sprang from the car. 'Taylor!' Aware someone might be listening, he clenched his jaw and forced himself back into fiancé mode. It was as ill-fitting as a second-hand suit. 'Mi amore—' He'd never said those words to anyone before and even knowing that they weren't genuine didn't make it any easier. 'Where are you going?'

There was a brief pause and then she spun on her heel and gave him an easy smile that probably seemed genuine to all but him. 'I was leaving you to park the car.'

He sensed her tension but didn't understand it. Hell, he was breaking his neck here to act like the devoted fiancé. 'It's parked.'

'You call that parked?' One eyebrow raised, she looked at the Ferrari. 'You can't seriously intend to leave it there.'

'They're lucky I choose to park my car outside their restaurant. People will pause, admire it and then want to dine in their restaurant to catch a glimpse of the man who owns such a cool car.'

'Or the woman.'

'This is a man's car, *tesoro*.'

'So defined by the idiot driving it?' Those beautiful green eyes narrowed in challenge and he was pleased to have broken through that seemingly impenetrable wall of control.

He decided to push a little harder. 'There is no way you'd be able to drive it. This baby has a six-point-three-litre V-12 engine with four valves per cylinder—' he glanced lovingly at the car '—and it hovers on the borders of legal. It can shift from car to beast in less than four seconds.'

'A bit like its owner.' Without waiting for him she strolled into the restaurant, those long bare legs drawing more admiring glances than the Ferrari.

She looked good and she knew it. He was fast discovering there was no greater aphrodisiac than a woman aware of her own appeal.

His own gaze fixed on those legs, Luca tried to cool the heat burning inside him and decided she and the car had more in common than she ever would have admitted. Both were high maintenance and both were eye-catching.

As he caught up with her he took her hand in his.

Her eyes widened. 'What are you doing?'

'Playing the part of your devoted lover,' he drawled softly, 'only my leading lady appears to have forgotten her lines. If I have to be engaged, then at least let it be to the woman who yesterday had her legs wrapped round me in the maze. Don't give me this bland, vanilla version.'

She blinked. Frowned slightly. 'This is who I am.'

'If I thought that for a moment this engagement would be off. I'd die of boredom before we hit our first anniversary and you'd burst from suppressing all that emotion.'

'Signor Corretti!' A man approached them and Luca felt Taylor tug at her hand, trying to free herself.

He tightened his grip and greeted the owner in Italian. 'I need a table.'

'Somewhere private?'

Distracted by Taylor's glossy lips, Luca lost concentration. 'Of course.'

'No, not private.' Taylor flashed her eyes, trying to transmit a message, but he was too busy deciding if those eyes were green or blue to translate the unspoken communication.

'I don't want an audience.'

'But I do.' She slid her arms around his neck and gave him a feline smile. 'Don't you want to show off our love to the world, honey?'

Luca, who had never been called 'honey' in his life, remembered belatedly that the purpose of being here was to be seen. 'You're an exhibitionist, *angelo mia.*'

'Says the man who just parked a red Ferrari in a no-parking zone.' Laughing, she trailed a purple fingernail across his cheek and he turned his head and caught her finger gently in his teeth.

Clearing his throat subtly, the owner of the restaurant beamed at them. 'I have a table by the water. So romantic and, on that topic, may I offer our congratulations. We are all delighted by your news.'

Determined to demonstrate that he could play his part as well as her and remembering what she'd said about conjuring up the emotions from deep inside her, Luca tried to imagine how it would feel to be engaged. Deciding that 'freaked out' wasn't going to help his performance, he swiftly ditched that advice and instead thought about the article he'd read. 'I am happy, excited and can't bear to be parted from her even for a moment.'

Smiling at an astonished Giovanni, Taylor urged Luca towards a prime table situated at the edge of the water. 'Your performance was terrible,' she hissed in an undertone. 'You should have let me give you acting lessons.'

'I don't need acting lessons.'

'You sounded as if you were reading from an autocue.'

'An autocue might be a good idea. I'm definitely not fluent in the language of love.' Luca sat down at the table and ordered champagne.

'Yes, about that.' She paused as the waiter fussed around them, waiting until they were on their own to finish her sentence. 'From now on, I don't want you to touch me.'

'*Scusi?* Are we or are we not supposed to be engaged?'

'We are, but I'm not into public displays of affection.' She kept her eyes down, adjusting her cutlery while Luca stared at her in disbelief.

'I'm Sicilian. We're an emotional, physical race.'

'Then hold it in.' Her eyes lifted to his and he saw something there he didn't expect to see.

Panic?

For a moment he was baffled by it, then he remembered the way she'd responded to him in the maze. 'Ah—now I understand. Enjoying sex is on your forbidden list too, and you are finding it hard to resist me, no?'

'No.' She answered just a little too quickly and then covered her glass to stop the waiter pouring champagne. 'Just water, please.'

Luca rolled his eyes and removed her glass, handing it to the waiter. 'Fill it up. She needs help to relax.'

'I do not need help to relax. I'm already relaxed.'

He waited for the waiter to leave them alone. 'I've seen steel cables more relaxed than you. You're such a sexual woman, and you hate that about yourself, don't you? You're trying to lock that part of yourself away and pretend to be something you're not.'

'I do eat. I drink if I want to, and our relationship is not about sex so that's irrelevant.'

'Let's hope no one was lip-reading when you said that.' He lowered his voice. 'Trust me, if we're engaged, there's going to be food and champagne and, most of all, sex. Lots of hot, steamy, very dirty sex so if you want this to appear genuine you'd better stop suppressing that side of yourself.'

Her cheeks turned pink as the waiter approached with her water.

'Thank you so much.' She gave a smile that turned the poor man into a gibbering wreck and Luca gave an amused smile.

'You're all promise and no follow-through.'

'I can follow through when it suits me.'

'And when is that? When you explode from holding it all in?'

Her fingers tightened on her glass. 'I'm not holding anything in.'

'You are suppressing so much, *dolcezza*, that when you finally blow the aftershocks are going to be felt back in your homeland. Don't worry. I'll be there to drag you from the rubble.'

She smiled. 'Do you think about anything but sex?'

'You're upset that I understand you so well.'

'You don't understand me at all.'

'No? Let's do a Taylor Carmichael 101.' He put his glass down and leaned forward in his chair. 'You long to let yourself go. I saw the way you reacted to my car in the first few minutes before you remembered you weren't supposed to enjoy fast cars. You long to drink champagne, but you daren't in case you drink a bit too much and lose control.'

'Is that the best you can do?'

'I haven't finished. You can't go anywhere without first looking to see where the photographers are hidden. You know they're part of the job but for some reason they make you nervous.'

She reached out slender fingers and took an olive. 'Are you done?'

'Not yet.' It was only because he was looking that he saw her fingers shake slightly. 'You don't trust anyone any more. You've locked yourself away. You won't tell me why so I'm guessing it's something you're ashamed of. Something you regret.' He watched as the colour drained from her cheeks.

Her breathing grew shallow and she looked away quickly. 'You talk nonsense.'

'I scored a direct hit,' Luca said softly. 'Now drink some champagne or the headlines tomorrow will be that you're already pregnant and that's the reason we're marrying. Neither of us wants that.'

After a moment's hesitation she picked up the slender champagne glass. 'To our future.'

'To lots of legal sex.' He glanced up as the waiter approached. 'Don't bother giving my beloved a menu, Pietro, I'll order for both of us. It will be a good test of how well I know her.'

To give her credit, Taylor kept her smile in place. 'But, sweetheart, you know I like to order for myself.'

'I know you do, my little cabbage, but I'm a macho Sicilian male and apart from that inherent trait that drives me to protect you from all things including menus written only in Italian, I'm suspicious of your ordering skills. You'll order the wrong thing.'

'I order what I want to eat, light of my life.' Her eyes gleamed. 'How can that be wrong?'

'You order what you think you're supposed to eat, kitten paws. That's not the same thing at all. A romantic meal out is about feeding the senses.' Enjoying himself, he watched her across the flickering flame of the candle, wishing they were alone so that they could laugh properly and enjoy their food without the audience. 'I refuse to order you a lettuce leaf. It would be criminal.' He proceeded to order in Italian while Taylor drummed long, manicured fingernails on the tablecloth.

Only once the waiter had left, did she speak. 'I can't believe you ordered for me. Dare I ask which unusual part of the anatomy I'm likely to find myself eating this time?'

Sending her a wicked look that brought colour to her cheeks, Luca raised his glass. 'To us! I'm much better at this than you are, by the way. If you like, I can arrange for you to have acting lessons.'

There was a brief pause and then she put her napkin down slowly. 'There's something I have to say to you, Luca, and perhaps this isn't the place but I need to say it so badly....' It was a voice he hadn't heard her use before. Soft, sultry and so richly feminine that the hairs on the back of his neck stood up. She reached across the table and took his hands in hers. 'I've never felt like this before. I'd given up on love. And then I met you and—and I didn't expect...' Her voice faltered and she looked puzzled, almost humbled.

The vulnerability on her face shocked him.

He knew she was acting, but the emotion in her eyes was so genuine he felt an involuntary flicker of panic. She was giving him 'The Look' and The Look was something he'd avoided all his life. He made a point of ending relationships before The Look was even a tiny germ in a woman's brain.

He tried to respond but his tongue was stuck to the roof of his mouth.

Her face was soft, transformed by love. 'I never thought this would happen. I never thought it was possible to feel love like this and then I met you and—' her breathing was fractured '—and you're everything to me. That's what I wanted to say. I love you. I've never said those words to a man before but I'm saying them now. I'm trusting you with my heart.' The look in her eyes was so adoring his muscles clenched in terror. She was so convincing he couldn't shake the uneasy feeling that crept up his spine.

'*Cristo*, Taylor, you're giving me chills.'

As the waiter murmured something incoherent and melted

away, the soft look in her eyes morphed into something harder and more brittle. 'Don't ever call me "kitten paws" again and don't tell me I need acting lessons or the next thing you'll be eating between two slices of bread will be a certain super-sensitive part of your anatomy.' As Luca shuddered, another waiter placed food in front of them and Taylor gave an appreciative sniff. 'Mmm. I can see wedded bliss is going to do nothing for my waistline.'

'Eat, *tesoro*. You can go back on your stupid starvation diet tomorrow.'

'I might not need to if the director can't be replaced.'

To another man her insecurity might not have been visible beneath the layers of polish and poise, but Luca had been raised by a woman whose insecurities had been welded into her skin.

Of course you're beautiful, Mama. Of course he loves you. The other women don't mean anything.

Unsettled by the emergence of that unwanted memory, he drained his glass and allowed it to be filled again. Why was he thinking about that now when he hadn't thought about it for years? 'He'll be replaced.'

'How do you know?'

'Because I know my cousin. He has many faults, but failing isn't one of them. He's too competitive. Now stop worrying.'

'Aren't you worried about your brother?'

Luca shrugged. 'Why would I be worried?'

'He ran off with your cousin's bride-to-be!'

'That's his problem, not mine. Now try this—it's delicious.' He spooned caponata onto her plate and watched as she dissected it with her fork. 'What are you doing?'

'Looking for its spleen.'

'It's vegetable, *dolcezza*. Vegetables don't have spleens.'

'This dish is vegetarian? You promise?' Cautiously she tasted a small amount and moaned. 'It's delicious.'

He watched as her eyes closed and she savoured the flavours. Her tongue licked at a tiny drop of oil on her lips. She was the most sensual woman he'd met and yet she suppressed it ruthlessly. 'Locally grown food and good olive oil. It doesn't come any better.'

'I don't want to know that it's cooked in oil. So are all Sicilian kids raised on this? Did your mother make this for you when you were small?'

Mention of his mother wiped his own appetite coming after his own thoughts on that topic. 'No. My mother wasn't the hearth and home type. She had other priorities.' He reached for his glass and changed the subject. 'Did yours cook for you?'

'No. My mother wasn't the hearth and home type either.' The poise didn't slip, but he heard something in her voice. The same dark undertones that coloured his own.

Her too?

They had more in common than either of them could have imagined.

'So what type was she?' He surprised himself by asking the question because normally he had no interest in delving beneath the surface of the person he was with and maybe he surprised her too, because she didn't answer immediately.

'The ambitious type. She had big plans for me.'

'She didn't want you to be an actress?'

'It was all she wanted.' She kept her eyes down so that all he could see was the dark fan of her lashes as she concentrated on her food. 'She was determined I would achieve what she hadn't and determined I would be the one to save the family fortunes. She was a single parent and money was tight. When I was a newborn she signed me up for work. I appeared in a daytime soap as someone's baby, then I played toddlers and so it went on. I worked right through my childhood. I didn't go to school—I had tutors on the set.'

'And you hated it?'

'No.' She stabbed her knife through a piece of asparagus. 'I was living every kid's dream.'

'Is that what she told you?'

Her eyes lifted to his and just for a moment he saw a little girl, lost and friendless. Then the look was gone. 'I had the most amazing experiences. I've travelled to places most people only dream about. Our house was always full of famous people.'

'So if it was so fantastic why did you fire her?'

Her face was white, her fingers shaking as she reached for her champagne. 'She was my manager and I decided she didn't have my best interests at heart.'

She was back in control, her insecurities masked by the poised smile she'd perfected. It was as if that unguarded moment had never happened.

'What about your father?'

'My father played no part in my life until he sold his story to the press when I was seventeen.' Lifting her glass, she took a sip. 'Are we done talking about me? Because the journalists outside the restaurant are beginning to create an obstruction. It isn't fair on the other diners. They have a right to eat their meal in peace. We should probably skip dessert and leave.'

Luca turned his head and felt a flash of shock as he registered the size of the press pack. '*Cristo*, is it always like this?'

'No. Sometimes it's really bad. Today is a quiet day.' Calm, she rose to her feet. 'Shall we go?'

Taylor walked through the tables, acknowledging greetings with a polite smile, hiding her dismay at the number of journalists hovering in wait.

Maybe it was tiredness, maybe it was vulnerability caused by the fact that he'd forced her to talk about things she didn't normally talk about. Maybe it was worry about the film part, but suddenly her control slipped and she stopped dead.

Luca took her hand. 'Ready? We need to look like two people in love as we walk out of this restaurant.'

'I hate them.' She blurted the words out before she could stop herself and he turned with a frown on his face. 'I can't face them.'

'Taylor—'

'They're like hunters, looking for weakness. When they find it they savage you.'

And they'd find hers.

It was only a matter of time before they exposed the one thing she dreaded them exposing. The threat of it had hung over her for so long she could no longer remember how it felt to live without it. It was a constant surprise to her that it hadn't come out before now.

Luca pulled her into the curve of his arm and Taylor gasped.

'What are you doing?'

'You give them too much power over you,' he said softly, his lips in her hair so that no one watching could lip-read or overhear his words. 'Rule number one, be who you really are. It's far more uncomfortable living a lie than living the truth. Rule number two, never let the enemy know your weakness. Now we're going to go out there and you're going to smile or not, whichever you prefer, but you're not going to show them that they scare you, *capisci*?'

His body pressed against hers, hard and powerful, and she realised that he hadn't been pawing her but protecting her. The way he'd angled his body had prevented the press from seeing her sudden panic.

Thrown to discover he was capable of sensitivity, she swallowed. 'I have no idea what *capisci* means but I assume it's some unspeakable part of an animal that you probably just fed me.'

The corners of his mouth flickered into a smile. 'Lift your

chin. The first rule of hiding something is not to look as if you're hiding it.'

'I'm not hiding anything.'

'You're hiding more secrets than MI5, *tesoro*, but now is not the time to talk about them. Now smile that perfect smile you've perfected—the one that tells the world everything is good in your life even when it sucks.'

Taylor smiled obediently and he took her hand firmly in his and led her across the vine-covered terrace, down some steps and onto the street.

His hand tightened on hers. 'You are thinking only of me,' he murmured, 'you're not interested in them because you're so in love with me.'

She just had time to mutter 'in your dreams' before they were mobbed.

'Luca, Luca! Can we get a picture of you together?'

'When is the wedding?'

'When did you first meet Taylor?'

There was no such thing as privacy, Taylor thought numbly. There was no question they wouldn't ask. No secret that they wouldn't unearth and expose. They had no limits.

She thought of what they didn't know and turned cold.

It would come out. It always came out.

She hadn't realised she'd stopped walking until she felt Luca's arm tighten round her. 'You've already had more than enough pictures of us together.' He spoke in that lazy drawl that made it sound as if he didn't have a care in the world. 'The wedding will be when we decide it will be and you will most certainly not be invited. Now go and bother someone else.' Gently but firmly he nudged her forward, deflecting the barrage of intrusive questions with casual charm as he guided her to the car.

She envied the ease with which he dealt with them and she left him to do just that and was just about to climb into the passenger seat when he threw her the keys.

'You're driving.'

'You can't be serious?'

'You've had one mouthful of champagne. I intend to take advantage of that. Not to mention the fact that you could barely keep your hands off the wheel earlier. Admit it, you're longing to take this baby for a spin.'

'One car is exactly the same as another to me.'

He smiled. 'Right.'

It drove her mad that he knew her so well after five minutes in her company. 'I'm not a speed merchant like you.'

That maddening smile widened. 'Of course you're not.'

Since her act was obviously wasted on him, Taylor slid behind the wheel, promising herself that she wasn't going to drive fast. No way. She was going to prove that a car like this could be driven sedately. She was going to prove he was wrong about her.

Luca stretched out his legs and rolled his eyes. 'Any time in the next century would be good.'

'I'm taking my time.'

'And while you're taking your time, they're snapping away,' he murmured under his breath. 'Snap, snap, snappety snap. Unless you want tomorrow's headlines to be Taylor Carmichael Forgets How to Drive, I suggest you make a move.'

Horrified by that prospect, Taylor pressed her foot down and the car roared and sprang forward like a racehorse out of the starting gate. 'Oh, I love this.' The words burst from her spontaneously and he smiled.

'So drive it. I presume you have no objection to speed on this occasion, my little petal? Let's lose them, shall we?' With a wolfish smile, Luca put his hand on her thigh and pressed her foot to the floor.

Taylor gasped and heads turned as the engine of the supercar screamed. The paparazzi jumped out of the way and she flinched back in her seat.

'Did I kill anyone?'

He glanced over his shoulder. 'Sadly, no. But if you slam it into reverse now and spin the wheel to the right you might just get lucky.'

'You're terrible.' She gave a snort of laughter and accelerated away, the power making her moan with pleasure. 'I've never driven anything like this before.'

'I can tell. Speed up. If they're going to chase us at least give them something to chase.'

'You're an exhibitionist.'

'This from a woman who ripped her dress at a celebrity wedding.'

'You ripped the dress.'

'And great fun it was too. I'm partial to naked thigh, particularly when it's wrapped around me.'

She felt a rush of relief as they left the photographers behind and she had to admit that the car was sublime. There was something illicit and wickedly good about the power she now controlled. 'Are they following us?'

Tilting his handsome head, he glanced in the rearview mirror. 'Strangely enough, no. Clearly they think we're off to have boring almost-married sex which no longer makes us worth following.'

'I wish.' She changed gear smoothly and he raised an eyebrow.

'You wish we were having almost-married sex?'

'No! I meant that I wish they thought we're not worth following.' Flustered by the way he made her feel, she shifted gear slightly too early and saw him wince.

'Premature gear-change, *dolcezza*. Keep her hanging on until she's desperate—then you give her what she wants.'

She felt her cheeks burn. 'Is everything about sex to you?'

'This car is all about sex and you know it.'

Taylor kept her eyes fixed on the road. She was trying really hard not to think about sex around this man. Quickly, she changed the subject. 'Thank you for what you did back there.'

'You mean when I chipped your frozen, terrified carcass off the ground? Want to tell me what that sudden panic attack was all about?'

No.

'It wasn't a panic attack.' Ahead of her the setting sun dipped low on the horizon, touching the sea and sending slivers of red across the darkening surface while the soft evening breeze whispered across her face and whipped at her hair.

It was a blissful, perfect moment and Taylor wished she could freeze time and keep things this simple for ever but that wasn't life, was it?

She was aware of Luca watching her, his expression veiled by thick dark lashes. 'You were scared.'

'Journalists do that to me.' Her hair tangled in front of her face and she pushed it away, hating the fact that her fingers were still shaking. She had so much to hide and deep down she knew it was only a matter of time before it all came out. And when it did… 'They wrecked my life.' And they'd wreck it again without a moment of hesitation.

'You mean they wrote stuff about you. You're too sensitive.'

'They wrote about private things. Things that were none of their business. And they lie—' The wind dried her lips and she licked at them. 'Do you honestly not care when they do that?'

'No. If people want to write about me they can go ahead. But I'm not ashamed of who I am. Unlike you.'

'I'm not ashamed! I'm—' She kept her eyes on the road. 'Private. People change. I'm not the same person I was at ten, or seventeen or even twenty-four, so I don't want to have to stare at that version of me when I switch on my computer or open a magazine. And yes, there are things I wish I hadn't done. Things I'd do differently if I had my time again.' Things she regretted deeply.

Her past lurked out there like a beast in the shadows and

GET FREE BOOKS and FREE GIFTS WHEN YOU PLAY THE...

Just scratch off the silver box with a coin. Then check below to see the gifts you get!

SLOT MACHINE GAME!

YES!

I have scratched off the silver box. Please send me the 2 free Harlequin Presents® books and 2 free gifts for which I qualify. I understand I am under no obligation to purchase any books, as explained on the back of this card.

❏ I prefer the regular-print edition
106/306 HDL FV9L

❏ I prefer the larger-print edition
176/376 HDL FV9L

FIRST NAME	LAST NAME

ADDRESS

APT.#	CITY

STATE/PROV.	ZIP/POSTAL CODE

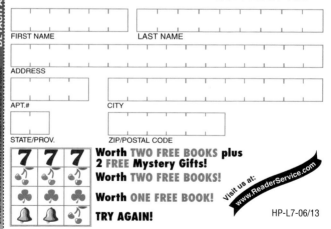
DETACH AND MAIL CARD TODAY!

HP-L7-06/13

© 2012 HARLEQUIN ENTERPRISES LIMITED
Printed in the U.S.A. ® and ™ are trademarks owned and used by the trademark owner and/or its licensee.

⊕ HARLEQUIN® READER SERVICE—Here's How It Works:

Accepting your 2 free books and 2 free gifts (gifts valued at approximately $10.00) places you under no obligation to buy anything. You may keep the books and gifts and return the shipping statement marked "cancel". If you do not cancel, about a month later we'll send you 6 additional books and bill you just $4.30 each for the regular-print edition or $5.05 each for the larger-print edition in the U.S. or $4.99 each for the regular-print edition or $5.49 each for the larger-print edition in Canada. That's a savings of at least 14% off the cover price. It's quite a bargain! Shipping and handling is just 50¢ per book in the U.S. and 75¢ per book in Canada.* You may cancel at any time, but if you choose to continue, every month we'll send you 6 more books, which you may either purchase at the discount price or return to us and cancel your subscription.

*Terms and prices subject to change without notice. Prices do not include applicable taxes. Sales tax applicable in N.Y. Canadian residents will be charged applicable taxes. Offer not valid in Quebec. All orders subject to credit approval. Credit or debit balances in a customer's account(s) may be offset by any other outstanding balance owed by or to the customer. Please allow 4 to 6 weeks for delivery. Offer available while quantities last.

If offer card is missing, write to: Harlequin Reader Service, P.O. Box 1867, Buffalo NY 14240-1867 or visit www.ReaderService.com

HP-17-0/6/13

BUSINESS REPLY MAIL
FIRST-CLASS MAIL   PERMIT NO. 717   BUFFALO, NY

POSTAGE WILL BE PAID BY ADDRESSEE

HARLEQUIN READER SERVICE
PO BOX 1867
BUFFALO NY 14240-9952

NO POSTAGE
NECESSARY
IF MAILED
IN THE
UNITED STATES

she knew it was going to pounce. Suddenly she wished she could keep driving into the sunset. Vanish and live a different life.

On impulse, she pulled in by the side of the road and stared at the view. 'It's so beautiful.'

'Sicily is the most beautiful island in the world. That's why I try and spend as much time here as I can.'

The phone in her bag pinged to signify a message, disturbing the moment, and Taylor reached across him eagerly and pulled it out of her bag. 'With luck this will be good news on the director situation.'

But it wasn't and her excitement turned to sick panic as she read the words on the screen.

Her hands grew clammy and her phone almost slid from her fingers.

She wanted to hurl it off the cliff, as if that simple gesture might cut her off from her past and keep her safe. But she knew there was no point. Whatever she did, her past would always haunt her. He would always haunt her.

'Trouble?' Luca was watching her and she tried desperately to pull herself together.

'No.' She shut off her phone and slipped it back into her bag.

'For an actress, you're a terrible liar.'

She knew she wasn't a terrible liar but she was fast discovering that Luca Corretti, for all his reputation as a shallow playboy, was sharp as a razor. 'I'm not lying. Just tired. I wish the press would disappear.'

'You care too much about what people think.'

'You have no idea what it's like.' The lump in her throat appeared from nowhere. 'No idea what it's like having cameras filming your every move from your first step to your first boyfriend. No idea what it's like to be betrayed by the people closest to you—people who are supposed to care about you and love you—and no idea how it feels to wake up and realise the only person in the world you can trust is your-self.' Her outburst shocked her almost as much as it clearly shocked him.

Taylor sat there, wondering how to pull back the words and recover the situation. She was usually so good at hiding her feelings but from the first moment she'd met Luca Cor-retti those feelings had been perilously close to the surface.

'Sorry.' Her voice was husky. 'Ignore me. It's been a difficult few days for me and today has been the most difficult of all.'

'Why are you apologising? For once, you were honest about your feelings.' Luca stared straight ahead, sunglasses hiding his eyes. Then he turned to look at her and when he spoke there was no trace of his usual humour. 'We should go. Do you want me to drive?'

'No.' She was grateful to him for not delving further but of course he wouldn't, would he? That sort of confession probably came under the heading of 'emotional depth' and Luca Corretti was a man who avoided 'emotional depth' at all costs.

He was no doubt already trying to find ways to ease himself out of their 'fake' engagement because who would want to be engaged to someone as messed up as her?

It took another ten minutes to get back to Luca's house and, as the car purred through the security gates, she spotted cameras and two security guards.

'You say you're not worried about the press but you have very high-level security.'

'That's to protect me from all the women I've upset. And all the ones I haven't yet upset, but probably will in the future.' He was back to his normal self, his tone smooth and bored, and was relieved he clearly didn't intend to question her further about her past.

'I would have thought you needed an army for that.'

'Fortunately for me I now have a fiancée.' The tyres crunched on the gravel and he sprang from the car and opened the door for her in an old-fashioned gesture that surprised her. 'I hate the word, but the institution might prove more useful than I could ever have imagined.'

'So now you're using me as a female defence system?'

'Something like that.' He relieved her of the car keys. 'You drive well for a woman.'

'That is so patronising. If I'd known you were going to say something like that I would have wrapped your precious Ferrari round a lamppost.'

The banter felt so much more comfortable than confidences but just being with him unsettled her. She was used to spending her time around ridiculously attractive men— men who spent their days working on their physique, men who spent a considerable time in front of the mirror, none of whom tempted her. Luca was different. He was spectacularly handsome, that was true, his Sicilian bloodline evident in his darkly brooding features and his volatile personality, but for her the attraction lay deeper. She was drawn to his self-confidence, his lack of pretentiousness and, most of all, his innate honesty. Luca Corretti didn't waste time putting a barrier between himself and the world and if they came too close, he simply shrugged.

As his arm brushed against hers she felt sensation flutter across her skin and float through her body. She was tall but he was significantly taller, much taller than her current leading man, who needed heel lifts and clever camera angles to increase his height. Luca needed no such help.

It was only as he closed the bedroom door behind them that she realised they hadn't discussed this part of their arrangement.

'Where am I sleeping?'

'In my bed, where all good fiancée's sleep.'

Keeping her expression in place she dropped her purse on the soft white sofa. She realised that she was exhausted. She hadn't slept well since hearing the film role was hers and now wouldn't sleep until she knew she hadn't lost it. 'I will sleep in your bed, but not if you're in it.'

'Sleeping apart is not one of the habits of happily engaged couples.'

'Unless you're expecting hoards of slavering women to break into your room tonight, I assume we're not going to have an audience for the next part of our deception?'

'We might. It would strengthen our story if Geovana deserves to hear you moaning with pleasure as she walks past the door.'

'I'm not a moaner.'

He smiled as he undid the buttons of his shirt. 'You'd moan if you were with me, *bellissima*.'

'Sure of yourself, aren't you?'

'I've never subscribed to the benefits of false modesty. I can have you moaning in under thirty seconds. Want to try it out? Practice the scene?'

Her heart was pounding. 'I don't need to practice. I'm a one-take wonder. And the only way I'd moan is if it was written into the script.' Her mouth dried as he shrugged off the shirt, revealing bronzed shoulders and muscles that could have featured in an action movie. The hardness of his physique contrasted with the effortless elegance of his clothes and she clenched her jaw and dismissed the thought that he was better looking than any of the actors she'd worked with.

'Admit it.' Fully aware of her scrutiny, he dropped the shirt over the back of the nearest chair. 'You can't stop thinking about that kiss.'

'What kiss?'

He smiled. 'How does it feel to spend your life pretending to be someone you're not? Uncomfortable? Frustrating?'

'I'm not pretending. This is who I am.'

The smile faded and this time when he looked at her there was no sign of the flippant playboy. 'No. You present the world with a plastic, perfect version of yourself. No flaws.

You show the person you think the world wants to see, not the real you. Maybe that's what some men want, but not me.' The hardness of his tone surprised her and she took a step backwards, wondering what had triggered that response.

'But this isn't real so what you want is of no relevance.'

'If I'm expected to spend time with you then it's going to be with the real you. The real you is the woman who was with me in the maze. That woman interests me extremely. Any chance she could come out and play?' His tone had lightened again but it was too late because already there was an electric tension in the atmosphere.

She was so aware of him, almost blinded by the raw sexuality that radiated from every throbbing, muscular inch of his powerful frame. From that silky dark hair to those moody black eyes, he was all man. And the most dangerous thing of all was that, somehow, he knew her. Not the public her that she'd created, but the real her. 'That woman is a figment of your imagination.'

'You had your hands on me. My imagination had nothing to do with it.'

'You had your hands on me first.'

'I never said it wasn't mutual.' Those eyes were dark as night, seeing everything she was hiding.

'It isn't mutual.'

'Sweetheart, you should know that I have a highly competitive nature and you're tempting me to prove it.'

'No.' She looked away from him, trying to snap the connection. Trying to pull together the torn threads of her protection. 'It was just a kiss. A badly timed kiss as it turns out.'

'Maybe not. We're here because of that kiss.'

'Precisely!'

Without warning he slid his hand behind her neck and drew her towards him. 'Once again we see things differently. You see this as a bad thing, but because of this situation I finally have the board listening to me and you—'

'I'm on a film that currently has no director.' His mouth was so close to hers she was afraid to breathe. 'How is that good?'

His phone buzzed and he paused, his eyes locked on hers.

For a moment she thought he was going to ignore it and then he let his hand drop. Instantly she stepped backwards, creating distance, and he gave her a mocking smile as he drew his phone out of his pocket and read the message. Dark brows rose. 'Apparently you do have a director.'

'We do?' Taylor's heart was pounding in her chest. 'He found someone? Who?'

'Rafaele Beninato.'

Just hearing the name made her feel sick.

'Are you sure?' It was her worst nightmare and the irony was that if she hadn't been caught in the maze with Luca, it wouldn't have happened. The first director would still be in place. But Rafaele had found a way to infiltrate her life, as he always had.

'His name is familiar. Didn't you and he have a thing once?'

'I—yes. But it was a long time ago.' She'd been seventeen years old and had been thrown out of the house by her mother. She'd been young, vulnerable and desperately lonely. A perfect target for a calculating opportunist like Rafaele. How had he got himself on the movie? He must have been stalking Santo Corretti as well as her.

Whatever the reason, her relationship with trouble had stopped being long distance and was suddenly right up close.

Luca glanced up from his phone. 'Bit old for you, isn't he?'

She was struggling to think. 'Is this the part where we talk about our past relationships?'

He looked at her steadily and then slowly put his phone down. 'I'll assume from your defensive response he was one of the ones who let you down. Is it going to be difficult to work with him?'

'I'm a professional,' Taylor croaked. 'I'll work with any-one I'm expected to work with. No problem. I'm just pleased to have a new director.'

'Are you sure?' His tone was deceptively casual. 'Because I can rough him up a little if you like. I'm your fiancé after all.'

She gave a choked laugh. Was it pathetic of her to wish, just for a minute, that their engagement was real and for once in her life she had someone who cared enough to offer sup-port? 'If you rough him up we'll be minus a director again. And I want to act. I must do this film.' Not just because the complexity of the role would finally earn her a reputation as a serious actress, but also because she didn't want to give Rafaele the slightest reason to use what he had against her.

Luca stared down at her for a long moment. 'All right. But he'd better not step out of line. I've met him a couple of times. The guy gives me the creeps. They want you on set at eight tomorrow morning to start filming the docklands scenes. He said he texted you but you switched your phone off.'

She hadn't wanted to see another text from Rafaele. In the past she'd blocked him and changed her phone but he always managed to find a way to contact her.

'I like to relax when I'm off set.' She didn't confess that she never relaxed because lurking in the back of her mind was the knowledge that her secrets could be revealed at any time.

Secrets that Rafaele knew.

And now he was back in her life.

Luca glanced at his watch. 'I'll drop you on set with a large fuss and dance and then pick you up later. And Randy Rafaele had better keep his hands to himself.'

He was seriously proposing that they spend the night to-gether? In the same room?

Suddenly she realised that she had more immediate prob-lems than Rafaele and that problem was six foot two of insanely sexy man.

'They have a trailer for me,' Taylor stammered. 'I should stay there. It's usually pretty luxurious.'

'There is no way I'm spending the night in a trailer for anyone, however luxurious.' Luca's appalled expression was almost comical. 'I'm strictly a five-star guy.'

'I wasn't inviting you to stay with me. I was suggesting we don't spend the night together.'

An incredulous dark eyebrow rose. 'People are no doubt struggling to believe I'm engaged. If we don't spend the night together the whole thing is blown. We'll stay here and I'll drive you. That's much more romantic. What's the film about anyway? I probably ought to know what my beloved is spending her day doing.'

Her gaze skidded round the room. If he wouldn't sleep on the couch then she would. There was no way she was sharing the bed with this man. No way.

'The heroine's husband was missing in Iraq, presumed killed. She goes to bed with his friend, gets pregnant and then the husband turns up alive. It's a film about forgiveness, I suppose. It's a very emotional role.'

Luca shuddered. 'Chick flick. Don't invite me to the premiere.'

'No chance of that. Do you have another room I can use? I need to read through the script if I'm filming first thing tomorrow. It's part of my routine and I don't want to keep you awake.'

'My routine is to have hot sex the night before a big meeting and I definitely do want to keep you awake.' His smile was slow and lazy, his gaze unapologetically sexual as he focused on her mouth.

She felt her limbs weaken. He was gorgeous. Too gorgeous. 'You're winding me up.'

'Maybe I'm not.' Dark eyes grazed hers from under long, sinfully thick lashes. 'Maybe I think you and I would be explosive together, Taylor Carmichael. Maybe I think we might as well take advantage of this situation.'

'Yeah, right—and tomorrow you'd sell the story to the press.'

'I'd never do that.' His voice was suddenly cold. 'Anything the press printed wouldn't have come from me.'

She thought about Portia and realised he suffered from the same problem. 'Doesn't it upset you? When women talk to the press about you—doesn't that make you mad?'

'No, because I haven't the slightest interest in what the general public think of me.'

'So what *do* you care about, Luca Corretti? There must be something.'

'I care about living my life the way I want to live it. I'm not a people pleaser—' his eyes mocked her gently '—except in bed. That's the one place I'm willing to make an exception to my rule.'

'Then go ahead. I'm not stopping you. If you can find a woman brainless enough to have sex with you then call her. I'd rather sleep in the spare room anyway.'

'No, you wouldn't. Admit it, Carmichael—you're tempted.'

'I'm so not tempted.'

'Yes, you are. But you won't give in to it—' his hand cupped her face and he stroked her cheek with his thumb '—because you're scared to death of being yourself with anyone any more. You are so busy holding yourself back you've almost forgotten how to live.'

Her heart was pounding.

He was supposed to be a shallow playboy so how did he manage to read her so well?

'I know this will come as a shock to you, but the fact that I don't want to rip your clothes is because I just don't find you attractive.' His response to that was to laugh and she pulled away from him. 'You are so arrogant. You just can't imagine there is a woman who doesn't want you, can you?'

'I'm sure somewhere in the universe there may be a woman who doesn't want me—it just doesn't happen to be you. But we'll see how long that self-control of yours lasts when it's really tested, *dolcezza*. You can sleep in the bed tonight. I'll take the sofa.'

And with that he walked into the bathroom leaving her fuming, confused and more desperate for a man than she could ever remember feeling in her life before.

CHAPTER SIX

THE SET WAS heaving with people when Luca dropped Taylor off the next morning.

He'd been intending to leave immediately, but he took one look at her white face and parked his car in a no-parking zone.

'Are you going to be all right?'

She turned her head to look at him, her expression blank, the dark shadows under her eyes telling him she'd lain awake for most of the night. 'Pardon?'

And Luca realised the reason she hadn't responded to a single word he'd said during the journey was because she hadn't heard him.

And the cause of her distress lurked at the edge of the set like a lion waiting for an injured impala to leave the safety of the herd and limp into the open.

Rafaele.

Luca knew the director was going to take one look at her pale face and see a potential victim.

With a soft curse, he unclipped his seat belt and she looked at him in confusion.

'What are you doing? You're going to be late for your meeting.'

Luca stroked her pale cheek with the backs of his fingers. 'I hope the make-up department on this film is good because you look like hell, Carmichael. Shame you're not making a vampire movie.'

'Make-up…?' She gasped and scrabbled for her bag. 'How could I have forgotten make-up?'

Because she'd been distracted. Scared.

Luca tapped his fingers on the wheel and thought quickly. 'I suppose I should apologise.'

'For what?'

'It's my fault you couldn't sleep last night. You should have just taken me up on my offer, *dolcezza*, instead of lying awake desperate for me.'

'Desperate for you?' Her voice rose slightly. 'You think I was desperate for you?'

'I know you were. You should have just admitted how you felt. There's no shame in finding me irresistible. It happens.'

'Not to me.' Two streaks of angry colour highlighted her cheekbones and Luca smiled and sprang from the car.

'*Bene*. Forget the make-up. You don't need it and he doesn't need to see you putting it on. You're ready.'

'Ready for what? Ready to kill you? You make me so mad I could—I could—'

'You could thank me. Two minutes ago you were the colour of mozzarella. Now you look human. Anger is instant blusher. So is sexual arousal, by the way, but I'll save that trick for when we're alone. And by "ready" I mean ready to face him.' Sliding his hand around her waist, he hauled her against him and lowered his voice. 'Never go up against a man like Rafaele showing you're afraid. Go out there and fight.'

Her eyes were wide. 'You made me angry on purpose?'

'*Sì*. Making a woman want to kill me is my special gift. It ensures they don't exceed their sell-by date.'

She made a sound between a sob and curled her fingers into the front of his shirt. 'You're—you're—'

'I'm perfect. Now smile—' he kissed the top of her head '—we have company. Not the company I would have cho-

sen, but such is life. Ah, Rafaele, I saw you admiring my car.
Work hard and maybe one day you'll be able to afford one.'

Rafaele ignored Luca and looked straight at Taylor. It was
like an eagle spotting a vole.

To give her credit, Taylor managed to look relaxed as she
greeted him. 'Rafaele.'

'*Querida*. We have so much to catch up on.' The sentence
was loaded with subtext and Luca frowned slightly and was
about to intervene when Taylor stepped forward.

'My name is Taylor.' Her voice was steady and strong.
'And we don't have anything to catch up on.'

'And soon she'll be Taylor Corretti,' Luca said coldly,
'so you might want to bear that in mind before you call her
"querida" or anything else that implies intimacy. I don't tol-
erate other men hitting on my woman. Unlike the wimp in
your movie, I don't forgive or forget.' He draped a possessive
arm around her shoulders, his eyes fixed on the older man's
face in blatant challenge. He thought of Taylor as she must
have been at seventeen and then looked at the man standing
in front of him and decided he didn't like what he saw.

Rafaele stepped forward, eyes narrowed. 'I read about
the engagement. I see her taste in men hasn't improved over
the years.'

'I disagree.' Luca delivered his coolest smile. 'Any time
you want to treat yourself to a suit that fits properly, just give
me a call. Well-cut quality fabric can transform even the most
unfortunate of body shapes. I'm sure we can do something for
you.' He could sense Taylor's tension. And something more.
Nerves. This man made her nervous.

Clearly her history with Rafaele upset her deeply and it
was obvious the director knew it and used it.

'I hope all this personal stuff isn't going to distract you
from your work. This is a challenging role for someone like
you.' With every carefully chosen word he chipped away at

the woman Taylor had become, exposing the vulnerability underneath.

Luca, who loathed bullies, resisted the urge to rearrange the other man's features. 'Taylor is the most talented actress of her generation. When you worked with her she was hampered by bad direction.'

Rafaele's lips curled. 'Taylor always responded well to direction.'

Luca stepped forward but Taylor's hand gripped his arm. 'I can handle this. I just want to do my job.'

'Good—' Rafaele gestured to one of the crew '—because today we're filming the scene where you discover the husband you thought was dead, is alive.'

'Obviously going to be a laugh a minute,' Luca drawled, turning her away from Rafaele and towards him. 'I'll leave you to it, *tesoro*, and pick you up at the end of the day. The board want evidence that you're real so we're going to a drinks reception at the hotel. Not my favourite way to spend an evening. I'd much rather be alone with you.' Before she could say anything, he cupped her face in his hands and kissed her slowly and deliberately on the mouth. The kiss was for the benefit of Rafaele but the moment their mouths met they were lost in it, the passion raw and elemental. He kissed her hungrily and she kissed him back, their surroundings forgotten, everything forgotten until the blare of a car horn cut through the sexual storm. Luca lifted his head, disorientated.

He stared down into her shocked blue eyes, saw his own confusion reflected right back at him and released her instantly. 'I should get to work....'

'Me too.' Her voice was husky and Luca, unsettled by how badly he wanted to kiss her again, backed towards the car and crashed into Rafaele, who made his frustration known.

'Look where you're going!'

Luca was too shaken to bother responding. Instead he slid behind the wheel of his Ferrari and started the engine, instantly comforted by the throaty roar. At least something in his life felt familiar which was more than could be said for his feelings.

He couldn't remember a time when he'd been so out of control with a woman. When had he ever before lost track of time or place? Never.

Pulling onto the road that led to the office, he told himself that he'd got a little carried away with his role. After all, she'd questioned his acting ability, so it was only natural that he would try and prove how wrong she was, wasn't it? He was as competitive as the next guy and any suggestion that he might not be convincing in his role as 'fiancé' was guaranteed to result in a performance worthy of Hollywood.

Having justified his behaviour to his satisfaction and confident that he had the situation completely under control, Luca relaxed.

He'd helped her deal with that slimy bastard Rafaele and she, in turn, could turn on her charm for the board.

So far their plan was working magnificently.

'So, Taylor, I admit we never saw this happening. Luca has never shown any degree of responsibility in anything he does. He's chosen to live his life on the fringe of this family.' The air on the sunlit terrace of the Corretti flagship hotel was thick with cigarette smoke and disapproval of Luca.

Taylor, who knew exactly how it felt to feel disconnected from the family you'd been born into, disliked the pompous chairman on sight. 'I'm confused.' She smiled her most feminine smile and had the satisfaction of seeing him blink, dazed. 'You say Luca has no sense of responsibility and yet he's built a staggeringly successful business worth a fortune.'

'Luca appears more interested in the models he employs than he is in taking business seriously.'

'I disagree. Luca is a man who works hard but also plays hard. He appreciates beauty. To be able to achieve the level of success he has achieved and yet still have fun seems to me to indicate a man who appreciates the importance of work-life balance.'

'Your defence of him is to your credit.'

'But should a man need defending from his own family?' Taylor was beginning to understand why they drove Luca mad. She glanced up and saw him surrounded by members of the hotel management team. He didn't even bother to conceal his boredom and she hid a smile because she sensed he went out of his way to live up to his terrible reputation.

And suddenly she realised what a clever strategy that was. Because he didn't appear to hide anything, no one looked deeper. No one suspected there was anything more to expose, which gave him an extraordinary level of privacy.

He lifted his head and caught her eye.

Just for a moment they looked at each other and the sexual charge was so powerful she felt the punch of it from across the room.

Her stomach tightened as she remembered the way it felt to kiss him and be kissed by him.

Turning away quickly she reminded herself that a kiss, even an exceptionally skilled kiss, wasn't trust. A kiss was a type of sensual manipulation. Trust was something different.

And trust was an indulgence she didn't allow herself.

Extracting himself from the group of grey-suited business-men, Luca joined her.

The chairman smiled. 'You'll be pleased to hear your fian-cée was defending you vigorously. We were discussing your addiction to beautiful women.'

Feeling Luca's tension, Taylor slid her arm through his. 'I'm thrilled Luca appreciates beauty.'

'Many women would be jealous.'

'Perhaps. But not me. We're with each other through choice. Love cannot be bound and held captive. It has to be freely given.'

Luca was looking at her strangely but he didn't say anything and the chairman beckoned to an overweight man in a suit. 'Taylor, this is Nico Gipetti, manager of our flagship hotel. You're his idol so he's been hoping for an introduction.'

Nico Gipetti's face turned scarlet up to his ears as he shook her hand vigorously. 'I love your work.' Having stammered his way through a stream of compliments, he turned to Luca. 'Any news from Matteo?'

'Not a sound.' Luca was looking at her mouth. 'But I suppose that isn't so surprising in the circumstances.'

The manager's features tightened in disapproval. 'What does he think he's doing?'

'I should think right now he's probably smashing his way through all ten commandments,' Luca murmured and then winced when Taylor drove her elbow into his ribs.

'What Luca means,' she said swiftly, 'is that he's probably keeping a low profile out of sensitivity to Alessandro's feelings.'

'So you have no idea when he will be back?'

Luca suppressed a yawn. 'No, but while he's away I intend to increase your profits by an indecent amount so I suggest you all relax and let me get on with it. I work much better alone.'

And why was that? Taylor studied him thoughtfully, wondering why he was so determined to keep himself apart, both in work and in play.

'It's a difficult time for the market,' Nico snapped. 'What makes you think you can do what we can't? You know nothing about the hotel business.'

'And that is precisely why I will make it a success.' Luca paused to study the cut of the suit of a man walking past, a perusal that ended in a disbelieving shake of his head. 'I don't come weighed down with preconceived ideas, nor am I working from a palette of ideas that have been used a million times before by both yourselves and the competition.'

The chairman joined in the conversation. 'Perhaps this is a good time to give us some detail. I'm sure Nico is interested to hear how you intend to add value to the brand.'

'That's easy. Your occupancy is down because you have no appreciation of style or beauty,' Luca said bluntly and Taylor almost laughed at the shock on their faces.

She loved his honesty. He didn't care what people thought, which meant he wasn't afraid to speak the truth. Working in a profession where people rarely told the truth, she found it a refreshing change to be with someone who spoke his mind.

Sadly Nico didn't agree. 'Perhaps we should talk in Italian so that we don't bore Taylor with our business.'

Luca scooped up two glasses of champagne from a pretty waitress with a wink and a smile. 'Taylor doesn't speak Italian—' he handed her a glass '—and unlike you, Nico, I have no problem with my fiancée expressing an opinion. I'd like her to be part of the conversation.'

They put him down at every turn and yet he was bigger than all of them, she thought. He had an innate confidence, a powerful belief in himself that resisted all their attempts to diminish him. They tried to make him look small and yet each time they knocked him down he rose higher, towering above them in every way.

She felt a flash of pride and then wondered why she would feel pride in a man who wasn't hers.

Unsettled, she sipped her champagne and asked the question no one else seemed interested in asking. 'So do you have a plan for the hotels, Luca?'

Luca didn't hesitate. 'We're going to refurbish the top six from the latest Corretti Home collection. Out with bland, hotel uniformity and in with style and originality. Instead of guests walking away with white waffle dressing gowns they could purchase from any retail outlet, they come away with ideas for decorating their own homes and recreating luxury in their everyday lives. They leave not just rested, but inspired.'

Nico spluttered over his drink. 'The Corretti name is already a strong brand. We don't need your help with that.'

Luca smiled. 'By the time I've finished Corretti won't be a brand, it will be a lifestyle.'

There was a stunned silence.

Nico hadn't touched his drink. 'You're assuming people would want your lifestyle.'

'How could they not?' Luca slid his arm round Taylor, who smiled up at him in full-on adoring-fiancée mode, but this time the act was easy because her admiration was genuine.

'So you're giving people the message that if they stay in a Corretti hotel, they soak up some of the Corretti style—that's a totally brilliant idea.'

A faint frown touched his forehead. *'Grazie, bellissima.'* He hesitated and then lowered his head and kissed her gently. 'And now I think about it, you'd be perfect to front the campaign I have planned. Corretti Hotels—First Choice for Taylor Carmichael, Movie Star.'

'I'd have to stay in it first, just to check it has my approval.'

His smile was intimate. 'Once the hotel has been refurbished, we'll christen the Presidential Suite.'

Her gaze collided with his. Her stomach twisted. The chemistry between them rocketed off the scale. Through the thick, lazy heat of sexual awareness she heard the chairman clear his throat.

'It seems Luca has extravagant plans for the business, but what about the two of you?' He beamed at them. 'You're just so perfect for each other. It occurred to us that a Corretti wedding would focus attention away from Matteo's untimely elopement.'

'Was it untimely?' Still looking at Taylor, Luca raised his eyebrows. 'I thought the timing was perfect.'

Taylor, still shaken by the depth of the physical connection between them, decided that goading the board was a sport to him.

'What Luca means,' she said quickly, 'is that there is never a good time for such a thing to happen.'

'Perhaps not.' The chairman didn't look convinced. 'But there is no doubt that your wedding would divert attention and give the press something positive to think about. You should marry without delay.'

It was a suggestion she hadn't anticipated and Taylor felt Luca's arm tighten around her.

'A rushed wedding would lead people to assume Taylor was pregnant and none of us want that.'

The chairman's smile faded. 'You don't want to be pregnant?'

'Of course she wants to be pregnant.' Luca's gaze drifted over the heads of the people around them. 'But not before we're married.'

The chairman relaxed slightly. 'The press is full of pictures of your romantic dinner together last night. Love has transformed you, Luca. A big family is exactly what you need. I assume Taylor will be giving up her career once you're married?'

Taylor choked on her champagne and Luca thumped her on the back.

'Taylor can't wait to have children,' he said smoothly as he gave her time to compose herself. 'To the world she's this fantastic, glamorous movie star but underneath all she wants is to walk barefoot round my kitchen, cooking my dinner and nursing my babies. She's a real earth-mother type, aren't you, *angelo mia*?'

Taylor had the feeling he was enjoying himself hugely. 'Babies—' she played along '—I can't wait. We've agreed on at least six, haven't we, Luca?'

'Six?' It was his turn to be startled. 'Of course, *bellissima*. I'm all too happy to make as many babies as you would like as long as you're sure you can cope with them while I'm away on business. Which might be often.' His sensual mouth flickered at the corners and she found herself looking at that mouth and thinking of the way he kissed.

'We'll travel with you, my heart.'

'*Bene!* I'll be working on my laptop while six adorable little children, all dressed in Corretti Bambino crawl all over you wanting you to read to them, play with them and tuck them in at night.'

The image he painted was so vivid she couldn't breathe. It was supposed to be a private joke but Taylor didn't feel like laughing. How would it feel, she wondered, to have a family like that? A family that supported one another? It wasn't a life she'd ever imagined for herself. Whenever she looked into her future she saw herself alone because any alternative scenario involved trust, and she knew she wasn't capable of that.

Sadness squeezed her chest, as unexpected as it was painful.

The chairman patted Luca on the shoulder. 'We'll leave you two young things to mingle.' Smiling benignly, he drew Nico away and Luca and Taylor were left alone in the crowd.

Realising that some response was expected from her, she gave a wan smile. 'I didn't realise you had a Corretti Bambino range.'

'We don't, but I'm just realising what an opportunity we're missing. I've finally found a use for children—I can use them to increase my profits. And the idea has potential to be expanded into the hotel group—a range of clothes to give guests the chance to make sure their child co-ordinates perfectly with their hotel suite. If we do it well, they won't even know the children are there.'

She knew she was supposed to laugh. She knew he was being outrageous on purpose, but the lump in her throat was wedged so securely she didn't trust herself to speak and the feelings were so unexpected she had no idea how to deal with them.

Registering her lack of response, his smile faded and he

tilted his head slightly. 'You're furious with me? I was joking, *tesoro*. I know you wouldn't want all that barefoot and pregnant in the kitchen stuff, but it was what they needed to hear.'

'Yes.' Her voice husky and she changed the subject quickly. 'Your family seems about as supportive as mine. Why do you want to work with them when you already have your own successful business?'

'Because they think I can't do it.' Luca removed her empty glass from her hand and gave it to a waitress. 'I have a congenital urge to prove everyone around me wrong. And I'm a Corretti. We were born competitive.' As he talked, Taylor felt herself relax and decided she was just tired. Everyone had strange thoughts when they were tired, didn't they?

'But you're not just Corretti, are you? You're Marco Sparacino's grandson.'

'Have you been looking me up?'

'Maybe.'

'*Non importa.* I looked you up too.'

'I'm boring, but your grandfather was a fashion legend. Right up there with Chanel and Dior. I read his autobiography, *A Life in Colour*. It was fascinating. What was it like growing up with him?'

'It was hell. He used to criticise what we were wearing. It drove my mother insane. No matter how she dressed, he used to tell her what she should be doing differently. It made her deeply insecure and she grew up thinking every problem could be solved if you were wearing the right thing.' There was an edge to his voice that made her want to delve deeper but it wasn't the right time or the right place, with people pressing in on them from all sides.

'I've seen photos of your mother. She's always so elegant.'

Luca's fingers tightened on the stem of his glass. 'Appearance was—still is—important to her.'

'The daughter of Marco Sparacino—how could it not be?

So how did you handle him? I can't imagine you did what you were told.'

'I got so fed up with my grandfather telling me I was wearing the wrong thing that I once turned up to a lunch stark naked.' Luca drained his glass. 'When he bawled me out I told him there was no point in getting dressed because he always told me to get changed anyway. He never criticised me after that.'

Taylor laughed. 'I can imagine you saying that. How old were you?'

'Nine, I think. I don't remember. All I remember was learning that pleasing people is a thankless task and you're much better off pleasing yourself.'

'But you made him proud. You've turned Corretti into something that people associate with luxury and elegance.'

'When I took over, the focus was on couture. I persuaded them to take a more integrated business model. We expanded into ready-to-wear and accessories and then we launched Corretti Home. Furniture, lighting, bed linen…' He gave a mocking smile. 'You can date in your Corretti dress and then go home and have sex on your luxurious Corretti sofa wrapped up in Corretti sheets.'

'Is that your tag line? Corretti—Bedlinen for Better Sex?'

'Not officially but I think it's possibly an improvement on the one we picked for the campaign. Thank you, by the way—' his tone was casual '—you were brilliant tonight. I haven't had a chance to ask how it went today on set. Did Rafaele behave himself?'

'It went well.' She chose not to divulge just how awful the day had been but Luca's gaze was steady on her face and she had a feeling he knew.

'If he steps out of line, tell me.'

'He's my problem.'

'You're my fiancée.'

Her stomach curled and knotted. And that, she thought, was turning out to be more complicated than she'd ever imagined.

A week later, exhausted after days of filming with Rafaele and sleepless nights in Luca's bedroom, Taylor slid a pair of dark glasses onto her nose, took a deep breath and left her trailer. Blinded by a storm of camera flashes she struggled to keep the smile in place and it came as a relief to see the red blaze of Luca's Ferrari. He was leaning against the bonnet, talking into his phone.

'No, I haven't heard from my brother. No, I don't have any comment on his behaviour,' he drawled, grabbing Taylor's hand and hauling her against him. 'I'm the last person to comment on anyone's behaviour….I don't have a comment on my own either because frankly it's none of your business.' He hung up and pulled her into him. '*Cristo*, you're sexy. How was your day?'

'Exhausting. I filmed the scene where my husband appears from the dead and discovers I'm carrying his best friend's baby.' And she'd worked harder than she'd ever worked in order to make sure no criticism could be levelled at her but still the director had managed to make her feel inferior with his constant sniping. He'd made her redo each scene repeatedly even though she knew it had been perfect the first time. He'd wanted her to lose her temper and she'd been determined to hang on to control even if it killed her.

'What you need is to chill or, better still, get hot and naked with someone and that someone is me.'

She found herself looking into sultry, sexy eyes fringed with impossibly thick, dark lashes and wishing she could do just that. And then she found herself wishing she could turn off her senses because she didn't want to feel this way.

Spending so much time in his company was creating a level of tension she hadn't thought possible. He was supposed to be a solution to a problem, instead of which he was becoming the problem.

Her instinctive response was to pull back but she was expected to play her part so when he flattened his hand against her back and drew her against him, she lifted her mouth to his. She'd intended it to be a brief kiss but his hands came up to her face and he kissed her slowly and hungrily. And because he was so good at this, because he somehow knew everything there was to know about exactly the right way to kiss her, she didn't even try to fight it.

Seduced by the heat of his mouth and the skill of his kiss, Taylor felt will power drain from her like rain water down the gutter. If it had been up to her she never would have stopped. Who would choose to end something so perfect? And in the end he was the one who slowly lifted his head and broke the connection.

Dizzy with it, Taylor looked up at him, expecting to see mockery, but he wasn't laughing.

And she wasn't laughing either.

'Let's get out of here.' It was the most serious she'd ever heard him and suddenly she was relieved she'd thought about this earlier before he'd fused her brain with the skill of his mouth.

'I've already planned tonight. I have a surprise for you—tickets for the opera in Palermo.' The idea had come to her halfway through the day when she'd been desperate to do something that allowed them to be 'seen' together, but still gave her privacy from the public. What better place than a dark box high above the auditorium? And it had the added benefit that she'd be saved from intimate conversation.

She had no idea if he even liked opera and no opportunity to ask him with the journalists surrounding them. One of them pushed against her in an attempt to elbow the competition out of the way and Taylor would have stumbled but a strong arm came round her waist. Holding her safe in the protective circle of his arm, Luca snapped something in Italian that Taylor didn't understand. Whatever it was that he said turned the man several shades paler and he backed away, giving them space, hands raised in a gesture of apology.

'Get in the car, *dolcezza*.' Luca was calm and in control. 'I'll get you out of here.'

Grateful to him, Taylor slid into the Ferrari thinking how much easier it was to handle the press when he was with her. He wore the Corretti power as lightly and elegantly as his immaculate suits but there was strength and steel under the casual sophistication and she knew the press found him intimidating. They treated him with a degree of caution they never afforded to her.

'Thank you.'

He didn't have to ask what she was thanking him for. 'I'm starting to understand why you're so scared of the press. They never leave you alone.' He was frowning as he weaved through the heavy Palermo traffic. 'Has it always been like that?'

'Yes. Right from the beginning. I had a mother who knew how to give them exactly what they wanted. She was the master at drawing media attention and using it.'

'Just what you want when you're an awkward adolescent.'

'It's got worse since then. I've come to accept I'll never shake them off. My dream is to go out and for no one to recognise me. Once, just once, I'd love to live life like a normal person, not having to worry about who is pointing a camera and how what I do will be interpreted. Can you imagine that?' She gave a short, desperate laugh because she knew it was never going to happen.

'What would you do? If you could go out and not be recognised—what would you do?'

'I don't know. Just go to a concert or something and stand in the crowd. Blend in. But seeing as that isn't going to happen, I choose to do things that give me some privacy. Do you even like opera? It seemed like a good idea but now I'm not sure.'

'I'm Sicilian. I love opera.'

She relaxed slightly. Even the most persistent observer was unlikely to interrupt the opera to ask them questions about their relationship, and the bonus was that they wouldn't be able to talk. He wouldn't be able to make some sharp comment that showed how easily he saw through to the person she really was.

He already knew far too much about her.

An evening at the opera should be perfect.

Except that it didn't turn out that way.

She'd thought that the dark would protect them from prying eyes, but it turned out she was wrong about that too.

Seated close together in the privacy of a box, his leg brushed against hers and she immediately ceased to focus on anything that was happening on the stage. She was aware of heads turning towards them in the darkness and felt a brief flicker of frustration that even here, in the protected atmosphere of the opera theatre, they couldn't escape the scrutiny of the public.

But that irritation gave way to deeper, darker concerns. Like the fact that although their engagement might be fake there was nothing fake about the sexual tension simmering between them. It was raw, hot and real and becoming harder to ignore with each burning look they exchanged. And the intensity of the feeling confused her. He was insanely handsome, of course, but she'd met enough handsome men during the course of her career to be immune to the combination of perfectly proportioned features and a powerful physique. No, the connection came from something deeper. Something she saw beneath the surface layers of eye-catching masculinity. And whatever it was that drew her, drew her now as they sat close together, thigh pressed against thigh in the dark intimacy of the opera house.

As drama unfolded on the stage beneath them, so drama unfolded in the box.

She was aware of every beat of her heart. Aware of *him* and when Luca's hand covered hers she knew she ought to pull hers way but she didn't. Couldn't. So instead of ending it there she laced her fingers with his and he drew her hand onto his thigh. It was a subtle, sensual dance between man and woman. Her gaze was fixed on the stage but she saw nothing, heard nothing, felt nothing except the strength of his fingers on hers and the hard muscle of his thigh under her palm. Heat traced her skin, desire knotted low in her pelvis and she opened her eyes because closing them left the world to her imagination and that was a dangerous place to be right now.

She'd promised herself no more relationships. She'd trained herself to ignore that wild, passionate part of herself that had got her into trouble in the past. She'd decided there would be no more unguarded moments where she trusted a man only to wake up the next morning and discover the personal had become public.

But this—this was more temptation than she knew how to deal with.

She'd chosen to wear a floor-length dress but that proved to be no barrier because somehow his hand was on her bare thigh, his long skilled fingers tantalisingly close to that part of her. She clamped her thighs together but the movement didn't dislodge his hand and she felt his fingers stroke inside her panties and her face burned in the darkness because she knew he'd find her already aroused. She turned her head and was scorched by the dark heat in his eyes. Her breathing was shallow and so was his and he held her gaze as his fingers slid deeper, exploring her with erotic precision and unapologetic intimacy until not moving took all her willpower. But she couldn't move or make a sound because that would have risked drawing the attention of the audience away from the performance onstage and so she was forced to stay totally still and silent. And he took ruthless advantage, relentless in his delivery of pleasure as he explored the slick heat of her, creating sensation so wickedly good she was forced to clamp her jaws closed to hold back the sound.

She wanted him to stop. She didn't want him to stop. She didn't know what she wanted but he knew and he took her there, with nothing but his fingers and the intensity of his hot, dark gaze that held hers all the way through the pulsing shock waves of her climax.

On stage the soprano was singing her way to the grave but here, in the shaded darkness of the box, it was all about life and passion.

Shattered and trembling, Taylor stared at him. He leaned in, bringing his mouth close to hers. His kiss was slow, lingering, deliberate. Personal. Less of an assault and more a promise and she realised there was no way this was over. His hand was still between her legs. Her hand was in his lap and he was painfully aroused, rock hard under her warm palm.

Time passed. She had no idea how much time until applause washed around her. For a terrible moment she thought they were clapping for her and then realised that the singing had stopped. The opera had finished. And she was expected to stand up and act as if nothing had happened.

It was Luca who gently eased away from her and smoothed her dress before the lights came up and she was grateful for the dress because it concealed how much her legs were shaking. She wasn't sure she was capable of walking, but he took her arm calmly and somehow she managed to walk out of the box, through the crowd, as if the passion had all been on the stage and not between the two of them.

There were stares, of course, but she was used to that.

What she wasn't used to was feeling so out of control.

Taylor kept her head down as they walked, ignoring the demands of the press to know when they were getting married, afraid to look at him because she had no idea what was in her eyes.

Flashbulbs blinded her as Luca accelerated away in the Ferrari and she was so relieved by the burst of speed that left everyone else far behind she didn't even snipe at him.

She didn't speak.

He didn't speak.

But the tension throbbed between them like a living force, thickening the air until it was almost impossible to breathe, the atmosphere sexually charged and the heat almost unbearable.

Their restraint lasted until they closed the bedroom door and then they both moved. Together. At the same time, mouths fused, hands desperate, tearing at fabric, sliding over skin, greedy for each other and determined to feed the hunger.

His jacket hit the floor.

Her dress slithered after it.

Her hands ripped at his shirt, exposing wide shoulders and hard male muscle, and she felt that muscle flex as he lifted her easily and flattened her against the wall. Her eyes closed. His mouth was hot on her neck and on the exposed curve of her breasts. He dragged down the lace of her bra and fastened his mouth over her nipple, the skilled flick of his tongue dragging a gasp from her. It was a relief to be able to let the sound escape.

She wound her leg around his hips and felt him shift slightly as he loosened his belt. Desperate, he fumbled for something and then his trousers hit the floor with the rest of their clothes and she felt the silken hardness of him against her thigh.

'*Ti voglio tanto*—I want you.' Switching between languages, Luca stumbled over the words, his hand behind her neck as he brought his mouth down on hers and captured her lips in a raw, explicit kiss that sent shock waves of sensation rocketing through her body.

'Me too—me too…' She was barely coherent as she closed her hand round the thick length of him, heard him groan and say something in Italian she didn't understand and then his hands were under her bottom and he was lifting her, supporting her weight with his arms as he pressed her back against the wall and entered her with a single hard thrust that joined them completely. The feel of him deep inside her was so shockingly good she cried out. No silence for her this time as the hot, hard heat of him consumed her and no silence from him either as he released a raw, primitive groan that originated somewhere deep in his throat.

She was already so wet from the erotic torment of their silent foreplay at the opera her body welcomed his, clamping round the silken strength of him, testing his control. She knew a brief moment of relief that he'd used a condom and then sanity left her and there was only the madness they created together.

'Cristo—' His voice unsteady, he thrust deeper even though deeper didn't seem possible because he was already part of her and they moved together, fast, hard, desperate as they let the feelings burn through them. Neither of them tried to stop it. Neither of them pretended this wasn't what they wanted, because both knew it was. It was what they'd wanted from that first moment in the maze. It was wild, but they didn't care. It was crazy, but they didn't care about that either. They cared about nothing except the moment and when the moment came, when he drove her to another climax, she pulled him over with her, her body tightening around his, sharing each pulse, each thrust, each explosion of sensation as they tumbled together over the edge and into ecstasy.

CHAPTER SEVEN

LUCA WOKE IN a panic.

The reason came back to him before he opened his eyes.

He'd spent the night with a woman.

The whole night.

In his bed. In his home, where he never brought anyone.

Admittedly, more than half the night had been spent having sex. Wild, abandoned, selfishly indulgent sex. After the first time when they'd barely made it through the door they'd graduated to the rug on the floor, his luxurious shower and finally the bed where each had exhausted the other until they'd fallen asleep wrapped around each other.

Wrapped around each other...

Drenched in panic, he was about to spring from the bed when he realised it was empty and that Taylor was stumbling round the room, snatching up her clothes like a woman running for her life.

Distracted by the urgency in her movements, Luca forgot his own panic and absorbed hers. 'Is Etna erupting and we have just minutes to escape? Should I call the emergency services?'

'Go back to sleep.' Dragging open a drawer, she locked her hand around the first item of clothing she encountered. Dressed only in her panties with her trademark hair clouded and tangled from a night of wild sex, she was still the hottest woman he'd ever seen.

Realising that for the first time in his life he was witnessing a woman who was even more panicked about relationships than he was, Luca relaxed slightly.

She pulled on the T-shirt without bothering with a bra, a decision Luca supported wholeheartedly.

'This is like a strip in reverse but it's surprisingly erotic.' His own panic fading, he hooked his hands behind his head and watched as she yanked on jeans in such haste she almost fell. 'Where exactly are you going in this much of a hurry? This is Sicily. No one rushes in Sicily. You're not on New York time now, *dolcezza*.' But he knew her frantic rush to get dressed and escape had nothing to do with a desire to get to work and everything to do with her need to escape from a situation that terrified her. It would have terrified him too, except that she was panicking enough for both of them.

'I'm going out—' she snapped the words and zipped her jeans so violently he flinched '—out…somewhere. Anywhere.'

She dressed with no thought and yet she looked effortlessly stunning. It occurred to him that women would break down and cry if they knew how little effort Taylor Carmichael put into looking as good as she did. She was thought of as an actress but she could just as easily have modelled, especially now with her expression as moody as Etna on a bad day and her hair pouring over her shoulders in wild disarray.

There was something oddly vulnerable about her panic and, because he understood it, he took pity on her. 'There's no need to run. I'm not about to declare undying love and try and put a gold band on your finger. You're probably safer with me than any other man alive.'

'This isn't about you.' She bent down to retrieve her shoes, the movement so fluid and graceful he immediately wanted to haul her back to bed.

'So why are you running?'

She came upright and scooped her hair away from her face, her eyes fierce. 'Because I don't do this. I—I just can't.'

'Do what? Stay and eat breakfast? Because that's all that's on offer.'

'I don't eat breakfast.' Her foot shot out and she kicked at the pile of clothes they'd torn off each other the night before, searching for something. 'And I can't do this whole morning-after touchy-feely crap. It's not me. Damn—have you seen my watch? I was wearing it last night.'

'It lacerated my back at one stage so now it's by the bed. And I don't do touchy-feely either.' His words didn't appear to penetrate because she glared at him as she strode across the room and snatched up her watch.

'Do you know how many years I've stopped myself doing this?'

'Quite a few if your wild response last night was anything to go by. Next time you might want to shorten your periods of abstinence. Your she-wolf act could kill a regular guy. I think I have teeth marks in my shoulder.'

The look she shot him speared right through him. 'So I suppose now you think you're a sex god.'

Luca discovered he was enjoying himself. 'You moaned, *dolcezza*. Despite everything you said, you definitely moaned.'

'So? It's a long time since I had sex.' Head down, she jammed her feet into her shoes. 'Don't read anything into it.'

'So you're saying any man would have made you moan?'

If looks could have killed he would have been a rotting corpse. 'I thought you didn't enjoy morning-after conversations.'

'Funnily enough I'm enjoying this one.' It was the first time a woman had been more scared than him. 'Admit it—last night was the hottest sex you've ever had.'

'God, why do guys need so much praise? Just shut up and let me dress in peace. I have to go.'

Luca smiled. 'All of this excess energy is wasted because you're running from a man who isn't chasing you, *tesoro*.'

'Don't call me that.' She spoke between her teeth. 'When we're on our own, there is no need to pretend we're anything other than—'

'Two people who share explosive chemistry in bed?'

'Not that either.'

'I fully understand your aversion to relationships. I'm having more trouble understanding your panic about a night of incredible sex. Is this because you lost control?'

'I did not lose control.'

'I enjoyed the opera by the way. I had no idea the whole experience could be so…passionate. I love to hear you moaning, but silent sex was surprisingly erotic.'

Her look was fierce. 'You took advantage.'

'I didn't hear you complaining either then or last night. You definitely moaned. And you dug your fingers in my back.'

'Are you finished?'

'For now. But only because we need to eat before we expend more energy.'

'We won't be expending more energy. This was a one-time thing. We're going to forget this happened.'

He should have been relieved to hear that from a woman. The fact that he wasn't surprised him. 'Fine by me. But any time you want me to make you moan again, just tap me on the shoulder. My skills are at your disposal.' He saw her eyes flash.

'I can live perfectly well without your skills.'

'Are you sure? Because it seemed to me that you were pretty desperate there for a while.'

'I was not desperate.' Without looking at him she slung her bag over her shoulder and made for the door. 'I'll call a taxi.'

Realising that she was serious, Luca sighed and sprang

from the bed. 'And spend tomorrow reading that we had our first row? You need to calm down and breathe. Give me five minutes in the shower and I'll drop you on my way to work as usual.'

'Not today.'

'Yes, today. Taylor—' he hauled her round and gave her a little shake, frowning slightly as he stared into eyes wide with fear '—this was just sex. Incredible sex, admittedly, but just sex. Sex followed by a lift to work.' He said it slowly, as if he were speaking to a terrified child. 'That's all it is, so don't allow the messed-up part of yourself to ruin everything we're doing here. You were the one who got us into this but we're in it now and we're staying in it for as long as it suits us.'

She wasn't messed up. She'd made mistakes and she'd learned from them and one of the things she'd learned was not to trust people. It was a simple rule and she'd had no trouble living her life by it. Until now.

She told herself that sex wasn't trust but she knew it wasn't as simple as that. What she shared with Luca was more than just sex. He got inside her head. He saw who she was.

And yes, she'd moaned.

Appalled with herself, Taylor paced the length of the bedroom and then back again. She could hear the shower running and she turned her head, wrestling with an almost painful urge to throw caution to the wind and join him there.

Admit it—last night was the hottest sex you've ever had.

'No!' She covered her ears with her hands to block out the sound of the water because hearing the water made her think of the man and thinking of the man made her think of his body and how it had felt to be with him.

When that didn't work she snatched up her bag in desperation and left the room.

Down in the kitchen she found Geovana removing warm

brioche from the oven. The scent was another assault on her already overloaded, overindulged senses.

Her stomach rumbled. 'Could I make myself some coffee, please?' She muttered the words in English and vowed to learn more of the language while she was filming here. 'Strong, black. Americano.'

Geovana smiled and responded in Italian.

Taylor caught one word that she translated as *breakfast* and shook her head. 'I don't eat breakfast.' But Geovana either didn't understand her or chose to ignore her because she loaded a plate with fresh, glossy brioche and placed it on the scrubbed, antique table in front of Taylor.

Her mouth watered. It was as if everything in this house was designed to tempt her self-control. She felt herself weaken. 'That smells so good but I really can't—'

'Granita.' Geovana placed a glass filled with frosted sorbet in front of her and gestured that Taylor should eat the brioche with the *granita*. Unable to find a way of refusing without offending, Taylor broke off a piece of the soft, warm roll and ate as instructed, intending to take only a nibble.

'Oh, that's so good….' She closed her eyes briefly, enjoying the flavour and the novelty of starting her day with food. She was so used to disciplining herself not to eat that she'd forgotten the pleasure of breakfast.

'Sex and food in one day. You really have fallen off the wagon.' Luca strolled into the room looking maddeningly fresh and relaxed while Taylor averted her gaze. He was the biggest temptation of all.

'I came down for coffee and—' She broke off as he kissed her and then stole a corner of her brioche. 'Don't do that!'

'Kiss you or steal your food?'

Judging from the way Geovana beamed at them both, she was thrilled by the scene of morning-after domesticity and Taylor was trapped by the story they'd spun.

Luca spoke in Italian to Geovana and helped himself to

coffee and brioche while watching Taylor. 'You don't like breakfast?'

'Of course I like breakfast. It's my favourite meal if you must know. Crispy bacon and a short stack.' Her stomach growled. 'I ran away from home once just so that I could eat it.'

'You had to run away from home to eat breakfast?'

'My mother decided that if I was allowed to embrace my appetites I soon wouldn't have a career.'

'So that's when you stopped eating.'

'I didn't stop eating but I learned to control myself.' *Until I met you.*

'But having to control yourself for every minute of every day is exhausting. Eventually your natural impulses escape.'

'No, they don't, because I hold them in.' Except she hadn't held them in the night before. She knew it. He knew it.

Taylor found herself looking at him across the table and thinking about the night before and maybe he felt it because his gaze lifted to hers and in that single split second she knew he was thinking about the same thing. Dropping her gaze, she focused on her breakfast, feeling intensely vulnerable. Not because they'd had sex, but because she'd been herself. It had been real.

And he knew it.

'I need to make a move.' She stood up suddenly and gave Geovana a faltering smile. 'Thank you. *Grazie...*' She stumbled over the word, embarrassed that her Italian was so limited. 'That was the most delicious breakfast.'

Draining his coffee, Luca rose to his feet, kissed Geovana lightly on both cheeks and walked to the door. 'I'll give you a lift.'

She would have preferred to drive herself but she knew that to have admitted that would have triggered questions she didn't want to answer so instead she followed him into the car, her heart sinking at the thought of another day of filming. She wanted to lose herself in the role but with Rafaele hovering in her line of vision it was impossible.

'So what's the history between you and Rafaele?' Luca accelerated down the long, tree-lined drive. 'You dumped him. Why the antagonism?'

'I'm sure your world is populated by disgruntled exes.'

'That's all that's going on here?'

She almost told him the truth but stopped herself in time, alarmed by the impulse to confide. She'd learned never to confide. Never to trust. She knew better than anyone that today's confession was tomorrow's headline so she kept her answer suitably bland. 'He isn't an easy man to please. He's very critical.' And he'd threatened her, but of course only she knew that. Only she knew what he was holding over her.

'These photographs are boring.' Luca scanned the images of a pretty girl standing on the sand with the sea behind her. 'It's like an advert for butter, not clothes. She's too wholesome. That girl has never had wild dirty sex in her life. Where's the edge? At the very least you should have stuck a huge shark in the water. We need something more contemporary and modern.'

'She is modern.'

'She looks like the girl next door.' It didn't help that he'd just had a night of raunchy sex with a woman he suspected might be half she-wolf. He turned away and stared out of the window of his office, thinking about Taylor.

She hadn't had much sleep the night before and she was expected to put in a twelve-hour day on the set with a director known for his childish temper tantrums and out of control drinking habit.

A director who was clearly still festering over the fact Taylor had once dumped him.

Making a snap decision, he picked up his car keys. 'I'm taking my fiancée—' he frowned slightly as he realised he'd managed to say the word without stumbling '—my fiancée for lunch. We'll meet again tomorrow to talk about the campaign.'

Wondering why no one else shared his vision for the new collection, he strode to the car and drove to the docklands where filming was taking place.

As a Corretti and Taylor's fiancé, he was allowed through the security cordon without question and he was about to ask someone where he could find Taylor when he saw her stroll through the abandoned docklands buildings, her hair flowing over an impossibly thin dress that floated around her slender frame. And he knew instantly that this was the image he wanted for his campaign. The contrast between decaying urban and floral femininity was exactly the look he wanted. Gianni had wanted a marine theme—docklands could be classed as 'marine.'

He was reaching for his phone to call Gianni and break the good news that he'd found the perfect setting, when he saw Rafaele striding towards Taylor.

Just looking at the way he walked made Luca clench his jaw. It was more of a swagger than a walk.

The man was a bully, a chauvinist and an idiot.

He watched, assuming they were about to have a conversation, and froze as he saw the other man grab her arm, spin her round and pin her roughly against the dilapidated wall of one of the old docklands buildings. Taylor struggled frantically, her fists pummelling his chest as he trapped her against the wall. She was twisting and turning like a madwoman and when Rafaele locked his hand in her hair, Luca felt a rush of rage.

Pumped up and furious, he abandoned his car, vaulted over the fence that surrounded the area being used for filming and sprinted towards her even as the director grabbed her face and kissed her.

Luca launched himself at the other man with an angry

growl, hauling him off Taylor as if he were a savage dog and delivering a solid punch to the side of his face. The director almost stumbled but then came back at Luca with a grunt. Within seconds both of them were rolling in the dust but Luca, younger and infinitely fitter, instantly had the advantage and he pinned the other man's arm behind his back and pressed his face into the dirt.

'Don't ever touch her again.' The blood in his veins pulsed with fury and he realised how close he was to the edge. Closer than he'd ever been in his life before. 'You threaten her, you look at her in the wrong way, and I'll come after you, *capisci*?'

'Luca?' From somewhere in the distance Taylor's voice penetrated the mist of anger. 'What are you doing?'

'I'm doing what someone else should have done the moment he touched you.' Springing back to his feet, he nursed his throbbing hand. 'I'm protecting you from him. Where the hell is everyone anyway?' He glanced round and saw people emerge from the fringes of the set, openmouthed and speechless.

'I was demonstrating a scene, you idiot.' The director stumbled to his feet, rubbing his bruised jaw with his palm. 'She kept getting it wrong.'

'If she was getting it wrong then it must have been because your direction sucked,' Luca said coldly, seriously tempted to knock him flat again.

'You shouldn't be on my set.' The other man stood there, covered in dust and fuming. 'I don't care if the producer is your cousin. You can't barge in here and disrupt filming.'

Dealing with a suspicion that he might have overreacted just slightly, Luca turned his attention to Taylor.

Her hair was mussed up and wild, her face as pale as an Arctic winter, her slender frame impossibly fragile in the flimsy dress.

He spent his days dealing with women who were considered the most beautiful in the world but in that moment he knew he'd never seen a woman more beautiful than Taylor.

And suddenly he knew. He didn't just want the docklands for his advert, he wanted Taylor. 'This is it.'

'This is what?' Rafaele snapped the words but Luca ignored him.

'This is the place.' Luca glanced around him, wondering why he hadn't thought of it before. 'It will be the perfect backdrop for the new Corretti collection.'

'Luca…' This time it was Taylor who stammered his name and Luca strode over to her and smoothed her tangled hair away from her face, worried by how exhausted she looked.

'I want to do the shoot here and I want you to model the clothes. We can link it with the film. It will be great publicity for both sides of the business. I'll talk to Santo.'

'Luca, you just punched Rafaele. And your suit…' She gave him a strange look. 'You're covered in dirt.'

Surprised, he glanced down at himself and realised he hadn't given a single thought to his appearance when he'd jumped the gates and wrestled in the dirt. 'There's a price to everything,' he drawled lightly. 'I wanted to stop him hurting you.'

'But it was part of the film. This is my work.' Her eyes skidded to the director and Luca felt a rush of emotion he couldn't interpret as he saw the look they exchanged.

It was a look of two people who knew each other. Knew each other well.

'You were struggling.'

'That was the part I was playing. My character is very conflicted about seeing her husband again.'

'You looked scared. Not the character, you. You were afraid of him.'

There was a few seconds of silence and then desperate eyes met his. 'I don't need you running to my rescue, Luca. What were you thinking?'

It wasn't what he'd expected her to say.

He'd expected gratitude, even silent gratitude. He hadn't expected criticism and he certainly hadn't expected that question.

What had he been thinking? Just for a moment his brain froze. 'I'm your fiancé.' He was relieved as the answer came to him. Yes, that was why he'd reacted in such an extreme way. He'd got so deeply into the role that he was actually starting to feel the way a fiancé should feel. What did they call it? Method acting or something. 'When I see you in trouble I'm going to try and protect you, and yes, I'm a touch possessive. Don't expect me to apologise for that. I'm Sicilian. We don't hand our women over to other men without a fight. If that isn't what you want from a relationship then maybe you're with the wrong guy.'

Her shock mirrored his own.

What the hell was he saying?

He didn't want the relationship to end. And anyway, how could you end something that wasn't real in the first place?

Freaked out by a nagging voice that told him he'd totally lost the plot this time, Luca turned on his heel and strode away.

'Luca wait. Wait!' Taylor sprinted after him, ignoring the sick feeling in her stomach that was her barometer of trouble. She knew a bucket load of it waited for her back on set but right now she had other things on her mind. Like Luca's extreme reaction.

She'd never seen him anything but relaxed. Even when he was driving too fast or drinking too much she had the sense that every action he took was deliberate, but this...

He'd been out of control, and if she needed confirmation of that then all she had to do was look at his suit.

Luca Corretti was never anything less than immaculate and yet his perfectly tailored suit was marked from his scuffle on the ground and there was a small tear in the leg of his trousers, no doubt caused when he'd jumped the fence. Jumped the fence to protect her.

Her heart was racing like a horse leading the field in the derby. All day she'd tried to block out memories of the night before but she thought about it now, her mind and her body remembering the intensity, the intimacy, everything they'd shared.

'Don't walk away—don't—' She caught up with him by the gate and grabbed his arm, releasing him immediately as he shook her off. 'Just...wait, will you? We need to talk.'

He stopped walking but his face was cold. Colder than she'd ever seen it. 'You just made it clear I'm not welcome on the set.'

'Because we're in the middle of filming, but—' She glanced over her shoulder quickly and his face blackened.

'So are you going to tell me what is going on between you and that guy? I mean, what's really going on?'

Taylor's mouth dried and her heart bumped hard against her ribs. 'Nothing.'

'This is me you're talking to.' His voice was thickened with emotion as he closed the gap between them. 'Last night we shared everything. Last night you were honest. Don't ever hide who you are from me.'

Was she the only one who thought this conversation was crazy? 'Last night was...' What was it? Taylor shoved her fingers through her hair, not knowing how to begin to unravel the emotions at play here. Not knowing which questions to ask or which answers she wanted to hear. Glancing over her shoulder, she checked no one was close enough to overhear them. 'Is this you acting? Because I don't know what's real and what isn't any more.'

There was a long pulsing silence.

Luca stared at her. Something flickered across his face. 'You were scared.'

She took a step backwards, shaken that he'd seen that when no one else had. 'I was acting.'

'No, that was real. You were scared.' He pushed and pushed, cracking open the shell she'd put around herself, seeing right through to the truth. 'I know you were scared and as long as he scares you, I'll be there to protect you.'

That statement ripped away another layer of her protection. 'Why?' The word was barely a whisper and it was a long time before he answered.

'Because I'm your fiancé.'

Taylor looked away quickly, horrified to realise she'd hoped for a different answer. 'You were…very convincing. Unfortunately you've also upset another director.'

And she knew just what that could cost her.

Rafaele was the wrong man to upset.

And suddenly fury mingled with despair. She'd been walking on eggshells trying not to upset him and now Luca had made things worse. 'Did you have to go to those lengths? You humiliated him. You made him look like a fool.'

'He did that with no help from me.' Luca was unrepentant. 'Why was he kissing you anyway?'

'Because he was demonstrating a scene.' She rubbed her fingers over her aching forehead, feeling crushed by the situation. 'If he walks out too, Santo will freak.'

'I hope he does walk. I don't like the way he looks at you.'

Slowly she dropped her hand to her side. 'You mean the fake part of you that is "engaged" to me doesn't like the way he looks at me? I think you just might have blown my film career by acting out a part we created in order to protect my film career.' She looked away from him because looking at him made her think of the night before and they were both in enough trouble. 'And what about you? You agreed to this to make yourself respectable. Does your board approve of a man fighting over his woman?'

'Of course. They're Sicilian.' But he was frowning, as if

something she'd said had given him pause for thought. 'I don't want to have blown your career. I'll talk to Santo.'

'No! You've done more than enough. I'll sort it out.'

Luca caught her arm. 'Tell me why you're scared of him.' His tone was low and urgent. 'Why do you care what that guy thinks of you?'

Her mouth was dry. 'Because he has…power.'

'Power? You mean over your performance?'

No, she didn't mean that.

'I just don't want more bad headlines.' That much was the truth. 'I just want to act.'

Luca stared at her for a long moment and then lifted his hand and brushed her cheek gently, his expression inscrutable. '*Mi dispiace*. I'm sorry if I made things difficult for you. That wasn't my intention. Go and finish filming that scene. There's something I need to do.'

Determined to make up for his momentary loss of control, which had clearly made things awkward for her, Luca spent the afternoon on the phone. By the time he drove back to the docklands to collect Taylor he was feeling particularly pleased with his plan so it spoiled the moment slightly to see her waiting for him, white-faced and tense.

'Your cousin fired Rafaele.'

Luca wondered why she thought that came under the heading of 'bad news.' 'Good. For once he and I are in agreement on something.'

'Rafaele is going to be furious.'

'And we care about that because…?' When she didn't answer, he sighed. 'Get in the car.'

'I'm starting to think this project is doomed.' She slid into the car next to him and closed her eyes but her phone rang immediately.

Luca tensed. 'Is that him?'

'No.' She relaxed. 'It's just Zach. I'll call him back later.'

'Zach? Who the hell is Zach?'

'Just a friend.'

'I thought you didn't have friends. I thought there was no one you trusted.'

'I trust Zach more than I trust most people, but that isn't saying much.' She dropped the phone back into her bag. 'What a day.'

Luca forced himself not to ask all the questions he was burning to ask about Zach. 'Does Santo have a replacement yet?'

'Well, that's the odd thing…' She pushed her hair out of her eyes. 'He's given the job to his PA, Ella. I've talked to her loads of times. She's crazy about everything to do with movie making which is why she's working for Santo but I never knew she wanted to direct. He's giving her the chance.'

'I'm sure she'll be brilliant. I'll even let her kiss you—in fact, I'll hang around in case she does.' Noticing movement out of the corner of his eye, he leaned forward and kissed her himself. 'Press approaching downwind. Look pleased to see me.'

Her lips were soft and sweet under his and he took his time, kissing her slowly and deliberately until she pulled back with a frown. 'OK, enough already.'

Luca, who was unsettled to discover he'd had nowhere near enough of her, reached into the back of the car and put a baseball cap on her head.

'Ugh—you'll ruin my hair!' She lifted her hand to remove it but he stopped her.

'Wear it,' he ordered softly. 'Put on your sunglasses. And for once in your life, don't argue with me.'

She was still staring at him when one journalist, braver than the others, approached the car. 'Taylor, do you have a statement on the fact that Rafaele has been replaced as director?'

'No, she doesn't.' Luca settled his own sunglasses over his

eyes, started the engine and rammed the car into gear but the journalist persisted.

'Any plans for tonight? Where will the two of you be spending the evening?'

'In bed.' With a dangerous smile, Luca pulled away and Taylor groaned.

'Thanks so much. Now the headline will be Taylor Carmichael, Sex Addict. Couldn't you have said something else? You could have told them we're going out to dinner. Why would you let them think we're going home to bed?'

'Because that's what I want them to think. I don't want them to follow us.'

'They always follow us. And you don't care.'

'Tonight, I care.'

'Why?'

'Because tonight, Cinderella Carmichael,' he drawled, 'I'm making your dreams come true.'

'My dream is to get on with my life without being bothered and you've just—'

'I've just made that happen.' Glancing in the rearview mirror, he took a sharp right and ducked into the private underground car park reserved for the executive team of the hotel.

He parked the Ferrari next to a battered, ancient car.

'What on earth…?'

'Move.'

And she did. But being Taylor she didn't do it without demanding answers.

'Where are we and what are you—?' She broke off and stared at the couple that had just climbed out of the battered, ancient car parked next to them.

'Give her your jacket, your sunglasses and the baseball cap.'

'But—'

'*Accidenti*, do you ever do anything without arguing? You are enough to drive a man to an early grave.'

'I'd haunt you.' Visibly confused, she pulled off the hat, the glasses and her jacket and handed it to the woman, who immediately put them on.

Luca narrowed his eyes. 'Not bad. From the back she could be you.'

'I know. It's seriously freaky. How did you do it?'

'I found a Taylor Carmichael double. She earns her living being you so she owes you a few favours.' He took off his own jacket and sunglasses and handed them to the man. 'Remember what I said. Straight home. Follow my security guards. You don't stop. Don't look at anyone. And drive too fast—that's what I'd do. You're sure you can handle the car?'

The man nodded and Luca sighed and reluctantly handed over the keys to his precious Ferrari. 'This had better be worth it. Is everything in the back?'

'Just as you instructed.'

'Then go.'

The couple drove off in the Ferrari and Luca yanked open the door of the battered car. '*Maledezione*, is this piece of junk even roadworthy? I've owned toothbrushes with more impressive engineering.' He hauled a bag out of the back of the car and thrust it at her. 'Put this on. And do it quickly before someone drives into this garage.'

Taylor opened the bag gingerly. 'A wig?'

Busy pulling on his own wig, Luca ignored her. 'I hope you appreciate the lengths I'm going to for you. Do I look hot as a blond?'

She glanced at him and gave a choked laugh. 'You look… unbelievably weird. The hair doesn't match the suit.'

'The suit! I have to get rid of the suit.' Reluctantly, Luca stripped off the exquisite Italian suit he'd changed into following his altercation with Rafaele. 'I can't believe I'm doing this for you.'

'Why are you doing this for me?'

'Because you said it's what you want more than anything

and I wanted to make that happen for you. I wanted you to have fun.' His eyes met hers and he saw the shock there and he knew she was seeing the same thing in his eyes because the only fun he was usually interested in having with a woman involved getting naked. '*Cristo*, you ask too many questions. Can't you just enjoy an evening out without dissecting it?'

'Thank you.' She whispered the words and there was a sheen of something that looked scarily like tears in her eyes as she stepped towards him and pressed her lips to his. 'No one has ever done anything like this for me before. You've made me feel really special.'

Luca jerked back, rocked by emotions he hadn't expected and had no idea how to deal with.

Maybe this had been a bad idea.

He had no problem with making a woman feel special as long as it was only for a short time, but he didn't want to make one feel so special she decided to stick around. 'Really special' sounded suspiciously like a warning alarm that in normal circumstances would have had him running. But he couldn't run because he was the one who'd arranged this.

'I'm not surprised no one has done it before. The wig itches and the car is unlikely to make it out of the car park.' Unsettled by his own feelings, which he had no intention of analysing, he took refuge in humour. 'Get dressed.'

Checking that there was no one in the small car park, she shimmied out of her trousers and Luca set his teeth. He wondered if he were the only one thinking about sex all the time. He couldn't look at her without wanting to strip her naked.

'I said get dressed, not undressed.'

'One comes before the other.'

He dragged his gaze from her long, slim legs. 'You're doing it on purpose.'

'Doing what on purpose?'

'Driving me crazy.'

'Am I driving you crazy?' She lifted her arms and removed

her top in a graceful movement, exposing her lean fit body. She was sexy and she knew it.

Taylor Carmichael didn't need anyone to reassure her. She made her own choices and was confident in herself.

'What would you do if I said I didn't like what you were wearing?' The question fell from his lips before he could stop it and she raised her eyebrows.

'You don't like me in my underwear?'

'That wasn't what I meant.' He wished he hadn't spoken and truthfully he could hardly concentrate. He was so hard his brain had ceased to function on any level above basic.

She looked at him thoughtfully. 'To answer your question, if you told me you didn't like what I was wearing I'd probably just take it off. Is that what you want?' Her fingers toyed with the lacy edge of her panties and his mouth dried.

'No, *Cristo*, don't take any more off. Put something on. Fast.'

'But you said you didn't like what I was wearing.'

'That wasn't…' His flesh throbbed and his mind blurred. 'Never mind. Just get dressed.'

'Maybe I won't.' She stepped closer and slid her arms round his neck. 'Maybe I'll tease you just a little bit longer. I still owe you for the opera.' Her mouth was a breath away from his and Luca felt his control unravel.

'Taylor—'

'Is there a problem?' Her lips curved slowly as she covered him with the flat of her hand. 'Because I could probably fix that.'

The skilled stroke of her fingers made him groan.

Her confidence in herself was as sexy as her body.

He'd grown up with a woman who needed constant reassurance and worked with women who were body obsessed.

He'd never met anyone like Taylor.

'I thought you were careful not to be caught doing naughty stuff in public.'

'We're not in public. We're in your private, high-tech garage with just your car as witness. And anyway, you're talking about Taylor Carmichael and thanks to you she's currently driving back to your palazzo. Which means we're alone.' Her hand slid slowly down his shaft and he groaned and hauled her against him.

'This wasn't part of my plan.'

'It's always good to be flexible. And talking of flexible…' She curved her bare leg around his thigh and he gave in to it and pressed her back against the car, breathing hard.

He looked deep into her eyes and then his hands were in her hair and he was kissing her and she was kissing him and it was exactly as it had been the night before. Exactly as he'd remembered it. The intense chemistry, the desperation, the clawing need that made him ignore the fact that his relationship with this woman wasn't following the usual pattern.

It was the wrong place, the wrong time and not part of his plan but his hand slid low and found the wet warmth of her and he heard her moan against his mouth.

A loud crash in the distance had them both pulling apart.

Frozen, they stared at each other and then Luca gave a soft curse. He would have taken her right there. Right then and not paused to think about the sense of it.

'Oops.' A strange smile on her face, she eased away from him and finished dressing in a flash. 'Maybe this isn't such a good place after all.'

'We could go back to the house.' His mind was a blur, his body rock hard.

'No. You've arranged a secret night out for me. No one has ever done this for me before. I want to do it.' She grabbed the bag and tugged on a pair of floral shorts. 'These clothes are hideous. Who chose them?'

'Someone with no taste whatsoever.' But it made no difference, he realised. Whatever she was wearing, she was the hottest woman he'd ever met. Trying to think cold thoughts, he changed into jeans and slid into the car, ducking his head so that he didn't bang it on the roof.

'Do you really think we won't be recognised?'

'I sincerely hope not or my reputation as the head of a fashion house is for ever destroyed. I would rather shoot myself than have someone think I chose to wear this. Come on. Let's do this.' Making an effort not to look at her, Luca turned the key in the ignition, rolling his eyes as the engine coughed and spluttered. 'Believe me, even if the clothes don't convince people, this car is a perfect disguise. Everyone who knows me also knows I wouldn't be seen dead driving this piece of garbage.'

Still laughing, Taylor was pushing stray wisps of hair into the wig. 'Do you like me as a redhead?'

In the process of reversing the temperamental car out of the garage, Luca allowed himself a brief glance. 'You look surprisingly cute given that you're dressed in something that should be banned by the fashion police.'

She pushed her feet into a pair of running shoes. 'Are you going to tell me where we're going?'

'No. It's a surprise. And turn your phone off just in case some nosy journalist is tracking you.'

Her eyes widened slightly but she turned it off. 'You're a very surprising person.'

'Surprising how?' He winced as the car bumped over the uneven road.

'Doing this for me. I thought you only ever did things for yourself.'

'I am doing this for myself. I want to have fun and you're no fun when you think people are watching your every move. Tonight you can be yourself. That's if we ever get there.' He pushed the accelerator but the car chugged along at the same pace. 'I'm starting to think that it might be quicker to walk. What is under the bonnet? I think someone forgot to install an engine.'

She clutched the seat as they bounced along. 'It must be killing you to drive something that doesn't go over ten kilometres an hour.'

'Next time I'll hire a donkey. It will be faster. How are you doing with that disguise? Have you tucked away all your hair?'

'I'm one hundred per cent redhead.'

Luca turned his head. *But still beautiful.* 'Scrub the make-up off.'

'You just kissed off the only make-up I was wearing. Where exactly are we going?'

'To a charity concert at the Teatro Greco at Taormina.' He could taste her lipstick. Taste her mouth. Distracted, he crunched the gears and winced. He hadn't had trouble driving since he was a teenager. 'You said you wanted to go to a concert, stand in the crowd and not be recognised. That's what we're doing.'

'I—seriously?' She sounded doubtful. 'I read about it and the lineup is fantastic but we'll be recognised.'

'No, we won't because we're not in the VIP seats, *angelo mia.* We are in with the crowd just as you requested. You are no longer Taylor Carmichael. Tonight, you are Teresa, a good Sicilian girl from a strict Catholic family—'

'You're kidding, right?'

'And I am Tomas, the son of a local farmer who is hoping to get lucky.' Luca flattened his foot to the floor to try and overtake a tractor but nothing happened and he rolled his eyes and made a mental note never to complain about his Ferrari again. 'We are sneaking you away from your strict parents, who would beat you if they knew you were out with me.'

'You're enjoying this, aren't you?'

Luca discovered that he was. 'Maybe I'm into role play. Think you can play the role of a virgin from Catholic school who has never been alone with a boy before?'

'Sure.' There was a shimmer of humour in her voice. 'Pull over and take your clothes off.'

'Shouldn't you be shy and nervous?'

'No. If I were a virgin from Catholic school who has never been alone with a boy before, I'd be desperate. So pull over and get your clothes off, Tomas.'

'If I pull over we'll never get the car started again, especially not on this hill.' Luca shifted gears as he drove up towards Taormina. 'How do you feel about pushing?' He winced as the car juddered over a bump. 'On second thought, forget that. You don't eat enough carbohydrate to have the strength to push a pen across a desk let alone a car up a road like this.'

'Are you questioning my strength? Because that probably isn't wise. I can take you, Corretti.'

'I wish you would. I've been desperate since last night and that encounter in the car park hasn't helped.' Ignoring the instantaneous reaction of his body, he kept his eyes on the road. 'Any time you want a repeat performance just leap on me and rip my clothes off. No prior warning needed.'

'I'm a good Catholic girl. I have no idea what you mean.' But she was laughing and he was laughing too, as the car shuddered to a halt by the side of the road.

'Let's walk from here. It will be faster and probably a lot safer. You do have the strength to walk, don't you? Ouch.' He winced as her fist made contact with his arm. 'What a hot, spirited little thing you are, Teresa.'

'Don't make me hurt you, Tomas.' Still smiling, she slid her arm through his and Luca frowned slightly and opened his mouth to remind her that they didn't need to play the role of an engaged couple tonight but she seemed more relaxed than he'd ever seen her so he closed his mouth and drew her against him as they joined the noisy, friendly crowd moving towards the arena.

He felt her tension as they were surrounded by people and

then felt that same tension seep from her as she realised that no one had even given them a single glance.

They didn't expect to see her and so they didn't see her.

And the disguise was good.

'So, Teresa—' he pulled her forward to the area in front of the stage where a group was already performing '—what does a girl like you normally get up to on a Saturday night?'

She blinked innocently. 'Normally I'm milking the goats, Tomas. And what do you normally do when you're not dressing in jeans that are a crime against fashion?'

Normally he was sleeping with some woman he never intended to see again.

Luca was slowly absorbing that fact when the crowd surged forward.

Instinctively he reached for Taylor, intending to protect her from the crush of people, but she was already dancing, arms in the air, joining in with everyone around her as the group on the stage revved the audience into a state of excitement.

As the sun set, darkness fell over Mount Etna and coloured lights played over the crowd and the atmosphere turned from excited to electric.

And still Taylor danced and it was the sexiest, most erotic thing he'd ever seen.

She moved with unconscious grace and sensuality, in perfect time to the music, thinking of nothing but the moment. It was the first time he'd seen her out in public and not looking over her shoulder.

'You're a real wild child, Teresa.' But she couldn't hear him over the music so he scooped her face into his hands and kissed her and she kissed him back, smiling against his mouth, happier than he'd ever seen her.

The chemistry was instantaneous and mutual.

Her arms locked around his neck and they kissed, oblivious to the crowd around them.

If someone hadn't bumped against them hard, they might

never have stopped kissing and Luca released her suddenly, wondering what he was doing and she was obviously wondering the same thing because her smile faltered.

'Thank you for this—' she glanced at the crowd and the stage '—and for arranging something you knew would make me happy. You've gone to so much trouble and, well, you've surprised me, Luca Corretti.'

He'd surprised himself. He didn't go out of his way to make a woman happy because a happy woman was a woman who wanted to stick around and he'd never wanted that.

But seeing Taylor having fun had given him a high like no other.

They stared at each other. He brushed her hair away from her face and she caught his hand and gave him a warning look.

'Don't mess with my hair, Tomas. Took me hours to get it looking like this.'

He'd forgotten about the wig. All his attention had been on her and suddenly he wanted to be on his own with her. 'Let's get out of here.'

'No wait—' she shouted above the noise, her voice pleading '—can we just stay for the fireworks? I love fireworks.'

He intended to talk her out of it but then he saw her face as she gazed up at the sky, as enchanted as a child as silver exploded against black, showering the night sky with a thousand stars.

They stayed until the light from the last fireworks had died away and then mingled with the crowd as they made their way back to their car.

'That was amazing.' She lifted her hand to remove the wig but he stopped her.

'Leave it on until we're home.'

'I'm not ready to go home. I'm not ready for this to end, Tomas.' Her eyes sparkled, alive and excited, and the rush of attraction almost knocked him flat.

'I think if your father could see you now he'd have a heart attack. What exactly do you have in mind, Teresa?'

She curled her fingers into the front of his shirt and pulled him towards her. 'I want to go to the beach.' Her voice was low. 'I want to go swimming.'

'Swimming?' Luca stared down at that full mouth and knew he was in trouble. 'Did you bring a costume?'

'No.' Her smile was all woman. 'But that doesn't matter because what I want more than anything is to swim naked.'

CHAPTER EIGHT

SHE COULDN'T REMEMBER ever having so much fun. She felt light, happy and...free.

Here in the car, protected by the darkness and the disguise he'd given her, she was no longer the Taylor Carmichael she'd created. She was the girl she'd left behind years ago. The girl her mother had disciplined into another version of herself.

The girl she'd forgotten.

'Tonight was the most fun I've had in ages. Thank you.'

She put her hand on his thigh. Felt hard, male muscle tense under her fingers.

'Carry on like that and you won't be a virgin for much longer, Teresa.'

'Is that a promise?' She slid her hand higher and heard his breathing change.

'I chose the wrong disguise for you. You couldn't pass for a good Catholic girl if I dressed you in a nun's habit.'

'How far is the beach?'

'Too far. I need cold water.' They were close to home and he pulled off the main road and they bumped and bounced down a rough track while she soaked up the dizziness of freedom.

'I can't get used to the fact that no one is following us.'

'If they do, they'll lose a tyre on this road and it will serve them right.' He switched off the engine and they sat for a moment, listening to the hiss of the sea as it hit the sand and the soft, rhythmic sound of the cicadas as they sang in the night.

The full moon cast a silvery light over the water and she decided she'd never been anywhere more romantic in her life.

'Come on.' She was first out of the car, pulling her T-shirt over her head as she ran down the sandy path that led to the beach. She heard him behind her and they hit the sand at the same time, kicking off shoes and stripping off the rest of their clothes. 'Cover your eyes, Tomas.'

'Why would I do that when the view is so good? I may be a simple farmer but I'm not stupid.' Without shifting his gaze from her he stepped out of his jeans. 'No wonder your father has kept you locked up, Teresa. You're a danger to mankind.'

Taylor undid her bra. 'I have a lot to pack into one night before you send me back.'

She dropped the bra on top of the rest of her clothes.

'I could be wrong but I get the distinct impression you really are thinking of swimming naked.'

'If I arrive home with my clothes wet my father will be suspicious.'

'True.' His eyes gleamed. 'In that case you'd better remove everything, Teresa.'

'Way ahead of you.' She dangled her panties from her fingers and saw his gaze darken but as he reached to haul her against him she dodged backwards and sprinted towards the sea, gasping as the cold water closed over her ankles.

How many times had she dreamt of doing this? How many times had she been tempted to run into the waves and swim naked only to stop herself because she knew someone would somehow manage to get a picture of her?

But tonight she wasn't thinking about that.

Tonight, no one knew where she was and she was thinking of nothing but the moment as she plunged forward and felt the cool water close over her head. She came up gasp-

ing and laughing to find him standing there holding a damp
mass of something unrecognisable in his hand. 'What's that?'

'Let's just say you're no longer a redhead.'

'Oh, no! The wig!' She made a grab for it but he threw it
onto the beach and turned back to her.

'Now you're finally naked.'

And so was he. She gasped as he scooped her up and
ploughed into the waves and tightened her arms around his
neck.

'Drop me and you're dead, Tomas.' But she knew he
wouldn't drop her and she buried her face in his neck and
breathed. 'You smell good.'

'Comes from spending the day herding sheep.' But his
voice was husky and, as he lowered her into the waves, his
mouth found hers. They sank under the water, kissing, desperate for each other.

There was only the moonlight but it was enough for her
to see powerful shoulders above the surface of the water. His
hair was slick and wet, his eyes gleaming in a face that was
so wickedly handsome just looking at him made her stomach flip.

'You're looking good, Tomas.'

'Taylor Carmichael skinny-dipping. Who would have
thought it? Finally the woman in the maze that day has come
out to play.'

Taylor Carmichael.

Her stomach gave a little lurch and just for a moment
she heard her mother's voice telling her she shouldn't be
doing this, that she should be thinking of her image, that she
shouldn't be trusting a man, but the voice seemed further
away than usual, barely a whisper, and when Taylor listened
again it was gone. Smiling, she pulled away from him and
plunged back into the water.

She'd waited too long for this. Too long to deny herself

this moment and as her arms cut through the cool water she realised she was smiling.

The moon sent arrows of light onto inky dark water and she knew from the soft splash next to her that Luca was adjusting his pace to stay level with her.

They swam until her limbs felt tired and her eyes stung from the salt water. Reluctantly she left the water, picked up her T-shirt and dried her face. Then she twisted her hair into a thick rope and squeezed out the water, conscious of him next to her. Conscious of every beat of her heart and the movement of her breath through her lungs.

She'd thought she was immune to this. She'd worked with hot men for her entire career and these days had no trouble resisting them. But this was different and she knew it wasn't his looks that drew her—it was his hunger for living. He ate it up, devoured everything life had to offer without regret or apology, and she admired that and wanted it for herself. She wanted to live like this every day.

Her heart gave a little leap although whether it was nerves or excitement, she didn't know.

All she knew was that she wanted him.

She pulled his head down to hers and his mouth closed over hers with no hesitation, hot and demanding.

He scooped her wet hair away from her face, his sinfully clever mouth fierce on hers, and she kissed him back with the same desperation, feeling something unravel inside her.

Instead of hearing her mother's voice she heard nothing but her own heartbeat, her own desires, and she wrapped her arms around his neck, her body aching for his, so aroused she couldn't think straight. She held nothing back, gave him all that she was as they kissed hungrily, bonded together by mutual desire and chemistry. She sensed that he was no more in control than she was and she heard him groan as she slid her hands down his body, savouring the feel of hard male muscle.

'You're killing me, Teresa.'

Laughing, breathless, she pushed him backwards and they tumbled together onto the soft pile of clothes they'd abandoned before their swim. 'I haven't even started. You're driving me crazy.' She licked at his chest, tasted the salt of seawater on her tongue and then moved lower until his breathing changed, until his hands tangled in her wet hair, until he took control and shifted her onto him.

She straddled him in the moonlight, her damp hair trailing over his chest, her eyes fixed on his as she took him deep, her lips parting as she felt the thick, hot pulse of his erection inside her. His hands gripped her hips and they moved together in a perfect rhythm as if this intimacy was something they'd shared forever.

'*Cristo*, Taylor,' he moaned her name. Her name. Taylor, not Teresa. The pretence had long gone as had the humour. His passion was every bit as dark as hers. They were both deadly serious, wrapped up in each other, oblivious to anything and everything but the moment as they rode the excitement until it exploded and took them over the edge and he caught her head in his hands and drew her mouth to his. And she discovered a kiss wasn't always about sensual manipulation. Sometimes it was a gift.

And as the madness faded she curled against him, her body dampened by sweat and sea as her heartbeat gradually slowed and steadied.

'I've wanted to do this for so long.'

There was a pause and then his hand lifted to her hair and stroked it away from her face. 'Swim naked?'

'No.' Her words were muffled against his chest. 'Be myself. Be invisible for a night. Be able to do what I want, with who I want, without thinking of the consequences. When I was a kid I just wanted to run off and assume another identity.'

'You didn't want to be an actress?'

'I loved the acting. I hated everything that went with it. And I hated that all I was to my mother was a meal ticket.'

'She was ambitious for you.'

'No, she was ambitious for herself. She was determined I'd live the life she'd wanted and hadn't had. She didn't want me to make any of the mistakes she'd made. She controlled everything I ate, everything I did, everyone I saw. Even the big Hollywood studios were afraid of my mother. She mapped out a path for me. She decided which parts I'd take, who I could be photographed with. And she played the media.' Taylor rolled onto her back and stared up at the stars. 'She'd start rumours, anything to make sure my name and face were always in the press. I felt suffocated. Stifled. The only thing I never felt was loved.'

'I'm surprised you didn't rebel in a big way.'

'I did.' She'd unlocked the dark and it came swirling over her. Shocked by how sharp and raw it still was even after so many years she sat up sharply, trying to push it back. 'I fired my mother as my manager and everyone labelled me as difficult. I wasn't. I was just horribly lonely and disillusioned about everything. I wanted someone to love me for me, not for what being with me could give them, but when I told her I didn't want her involved in my work any more, she told me to move out. And she gave all these stories to the press about how I'd betrayed her.' The agony was as raw as ever. 'She was my mom, but she was only ever interested in what she could get from being with me. And I soon learned that was true of everyone around me. There was no one I could trust.' She didn't give him the detail. Didn't spell out the embarrassing number of times she'd trusted a person only to find intimate details in the press the next day.

'Where did you go?'

Taylor wrapped her arms around her knees. 'I moved in with Rafaele. He was directing my film and he saw me falling apart under the pressure. He offered me somewhere to go.'

'In other words he took advantage.'

'It didn't seem that way at the time but yes. I made a bad decision. I was seventeen and up until that point my mother had made virtually every decision for me.' She could see now that she'd allowed her vulnerability to colour her view of the people around her. 'I was so lonely. So desperate for someone who would love me for myself and not for what they'd gain from being with me. The breakup with my mother was all over the press. It was horrible. And that was when my father saw his opportunity to come back into my life and play the hero.'

'Perfect timing.'

'Yes. Except I was pretty messed up by then. I couldn't see why he would want me when he hadn't bothered being in my life for the first seventeen years and I told him that. So then he milked the press interest for everything it was worth and told more stories about me being a spoiled brat. I kept the media going single-handed. Every day there was another story about me. It was vile. The only person who seemed to care about me was Rafaele.'

Luca took her hand in the dark. 'Bastard.'

It was exactly the right response. She didn't think she could have handled sympathy, although the strength of his fingers on hers felt good.

'Yes. He wasn't a nice man.' This was when she should tell him. She should confess about the phone calls, the threats, the sick feeling she lived with every day, the stuff she was terrified of people discovering, but she'd kept her secret for too long to part with it now.

Trust, even this degree of trust, was so new to her it felt unfamiliar so she drew her hand away from his. 'Enough of that. Tonight is about having fun.'

And she realised with a lurch that every moment she'd spent with him had been fun. Even when they were fighting, he made her laugh. Unsettled by that realisation, she lightened her tone. 'Good job the board can't see you now lying naked on a public beach. I think you're newfound respectability just died a death, Corretti.'

'What the board doesn't see the board can't moan about. And it isn't a public beach.' He wrapped his arms around her and hauled her back to him, showing no urgency to get dressed, and she relaxed against him. Why not? It was perfect lying here with only the sounds of the sea for company.

'What do you mean? If it isn't public, what are we doing here?'

'It's my beach. Private. There's a path that leads up to the house from here.'

'Seriously?' She lifted her head and stared at him through the semi-darkness. 'We're that close? So we could leave the car and just walk?'

'If you want to. But it's not easy to follow in the dark and it's steep. Car would be faster.'

'Then let's take the car.' Suddenly she wanted to be home with him and she sprang to her feet and tugged her clothes out from under him. 'I have no idea what happened to the wig.'

'Doesn't matter. It served its purpose.' The serious nature of their conversation forgotten, he took her hand and they sprinted back to the car.

Taylor sat, covered in sand and happiness, wishing her life could always be like this.

'I enjoyed being Teresa. It was fun.' And she rarely did anything for fun. Fun wasn't part of her plan.

'Having fun suits you. You were built to have fun.' He shot out a hand to steady her as the car lurched up the road. 'Only next time let's have fun in the Ferrari. I don't mind buying you a wig but I draw the line at driving this car again.'

'Where is the Ferrari?'

'Hopefully back in the garage with no damage to the paintwork.'

'I'm covered in sand. What if Geovana sees us?'

'She'll thoroughly approve, but I'd rather avoid that conversation if possible.'

Like naughty children, they sneaked into the house, trailing sand on polished wood.

'We are going to be in trouble tomorrow.' She gasped as Luca nudged her into the shower, removed her clothes for the second time in one evening and turned on the jets.

'Then it's a good thing I've never been frightened of trouble.'

Taylor opened her mouth to ask what would happen when everyone found out their relationship was fake, but then closed it again.

Tonight, she didn't want to think that this was fake. And this part wasn't, was it? The engagement—sure, that was fake. But everything else?

No, not this part, with his hands in her hair and his mouth hot and demanding on hers. This was definitely real, and she closed her eyes and let the water wash over her. Felt his hands move lower, gasped at the skilled slide of his fingers over the most sensitive parts of her and after that she stopped thinking at all and just let herself feel.

They fell into a routine—work during the day and each other at night. Neither of them used the word *relationship*, nor any other word that might have implied their arrangement had in any way veered from the original plan.

Taylor found working with Ella, the new director, fulfilling and fun.

Of Rafaele she'd heard nothing and even her phone was silent.

She started to relax for the first time in years. It occurred to her that maybe Luca had frightened him off.

And although she and Luca kept up their public appearances, he was remarkably good at protecting her privacy and giving her space.

164 AN INVITATION TO SIN

It was several weeks after Rafaele's departure when she woke one morning to find herself alone in the bed.

Luca was standing on the balcony of the bedroom wearing nothing but a pair of hastily pulled-on jeans, nursing a cup of strong coffee as he stared into the distance.

Taylor slid out of bed and walked over to him. 'You have the board meeting today. Is that why you're awake?'

'I'm enjoying a few moments of smug satisfaction that my interior make-over has had such an impact on profits. Profits of Corretti Home are up by thirty per cent and I have a team working on a strategy for Corretti Bambino. Would it make you laugh to discover I was studying population forecasts yesterday?'

She laughed and slid her arms round his waist, enjoying the peace and the privacy. 'Have you always lived in Sicily? Did you grow up in this house?'

'No.'

His lack of response frustrated her and she drew away slightly. 'You never tell me anything about yourself.'

'There's nothing to say.'

'Of course there isn't. You had no life before you met me.' She kept her voice cool and his hand shot out and he hauled her back so that she was eye to eye with him.

'Don't do that. Don't pretend you don't care and that I haven't just hurt your feelings.' His voice was rough and sexy, his jaw dark with stubble. 'Don't tuck the real you back inside the fake you. It's too much effort to dig her out again, but if I have to I will, because there's only one version of Taylor that interests me.'

'Fine! If you want honesty I'll give you honesty. Yes, it hurts my feelings when you strip me naked and have sex with me all night, every night, and then won't answer a single question about yourself.'

They were eye to eye, nose to nose, flat up against each

other and she could feel the warmth of his chest against her skin.

And then he released her and raked his fingers through his hair. 'Get dressed.' His voice was unsteady and she felt a sudden lurch of horror.

Was this it?

Was this the end of their 'engagement'? Had he decided that now his project was safely reaching a satisfactory conclusion he no longer needed her?

'Why do you want me to get dressed?'

'I'm taking you to meet someone.'

Luca parked the car outside the house and questioned the impulse that had driven him to bring a woman to a place he'd never brought a woman to before.

As if realising something significant was happening, Taylor gave him a puzzled look. 'Where are we?'

'This is my grandmother's house.'

'You visit your grandmother?'

Luca strolled round the car and opened the door for her. 'What's wrong with that?'

'Nothing but—' she bit her lip '—I'm just surprised, that's all. You don't strike me as the sort of guy who visits his grandmother. I thought your family wasn't close.'

'We're not. But my grandmother makes my life hell if I don't drop in and see her once in a while. She's heard news of our engagement. She wants to meet you. I'd appreciate it if you'd play the role of loving fiancée. She doesn't need to know our relationship consists of numerous fake performances and endless nights of hot sex.'

Endless nights?

The realisation hit him in the gut and he frowned slightly but Taylor didn't comment on that.

'You care about her.'

Luca shrugged. 'I don't want to upset her. She lost my

grandfather a few months ago. I try and visit whenever I'm not travelling. She'll be on the terrace at this time, eating breakfast.'

With Taylor's hand locked in his, he strode round the house to the vine-covered terrace and found his grandmother sipping coffee.

Every time he came here, the memories came with him but he'd already stayed away too long and he greeted her in Italian and stooped to kiss her wrinkled cheek. 'I brought Taylor to meet you, Nonna.'

'And about time too. Come and sit down.' His grandmother spoke in accented English and gestured to the chair next to her. 'I want to see the woman who finally stole the heart of my favourite grandson.'

'We're all her favourite grandson.' Knowing how wary Taylor was with people she didn't know Luca wondered if the barriers would come up, but she sank into the chair and faced the old lady with a smile.

'My Italian is terrible. I apologise. And I know how to say that…' She faltered slightly. *'Mi dispiace.'*

'No doubt you and Luca are finding other ways to communicate.' The old lady's eyes gleamed and Taylor laughed.

'His English is fluent.'

'Yes. He always was the cleverest of my grandsons. He just hid it well. So his reputation with women doesn't seem to frighten you.'

'I have a reputation of my own.'

'So I understand. You're the girl who fired her own mother.' His grandmother peered at her and Luca cursed under his breath, knowing how fiercely Taylor guarded her privacy.

'Nonna—'

'Yes, I did.' Taylor's voice was steady. 'She used me as a way of making money. She didn't care about what I wanted or what I needed. She wasn't good for me.'

Braced to defend Taylor from a lecture on the importance of family, Luca watched in surprise as his grandmother took Taylor's hands in hers. 'Family should be about giving unselfish support and that is particularly true of the bond between a mother and child. I'm glad you had the strength to remove her from your life. You obviously showed remarkably good judgement for someone that young. So tell me what you love about my Luca.'

'Nonna—' Cursing under his breath, Luca tried to interrupt but Taylor answered without hesitation.

'Lots of things. I love his sense of humour, his strength and the fact that he's proud of who he is. I envy that. I...' She hesitated. 'I want to be more like that. I'm trying to be more like that. It isn't easy.'

'You're an actress. Fortunately my grandson is used to drama. He was raised on it.' His grandmother gave him a meaningful look and Luca switched to Italian.

'I don't want to talk about that.'

'I know. You never do.' Her voice soft, his grandmother reached out to him and he frowned as he stared down at her wrinkled hands locked tightly around his.

'Nonna—'

'You'll be perfect together. I sense it.' She patted his hands and then released them. 'And now you'll stay and eat breakfast with me.'

They stayed for an hour, an hour during which Taylor talked about growing up in America, about her mother's ambition and her father's reappearance once she'd started earning big money.

'I want you to come and see me often.' The old lady patted Taylor's hand. 'Luca calls me Nonna, but if you prefer you can call me Teresa.'

'Teresa?' Startled, Taylor glanced up at him and Luca gave a dismissive shrug.

'It's a good name.'

She didn't speak until they were safely inside the car. 'I thought Teresa was some random name you picked and it turns out it's your grandmother's name and she's this wonderful, amazing person.' The choke in her voice surprised him. He was so used to her hiding her real feelings that this new Taylor unsettled him.

'She liked you a lot.'

'She'll hate me when she finds out this is fake.'

'It's me she'll be angry with.'

'I wouldn't be so sure about that. She adores you. I didn't even know you had a grandmother. What did she mean that you were raised on drama?'

'We're Sicilian. Drama is in the genes. Why be calm when you can explode?' But he could see his smooth response hadn't fooled her and the tension of the morning reappeared.

'You never talk about your childhood. You've never told me anything.'

'I've never been one to coo over old baby photographs.' Luca felt sweat prickle at the back of his neck and started the engine. 'Let's go.'

'What was your mother like?'

He kept his eyes on the road. 'She was very beautiful. Still is.'

'I wasn't asking you what she looks like—I know she's beautiful, I've seen pictures. I was asking what she was like as a mother.' There was a wistfulness to her voice. 'What is she like as a person?'

Desperately insecure, volatile, a danger to herself. 'Why do you want to know?'

'I'm just interested. I guess I'm wondering why you're so freaked out about relationships. Is she the reason?'

He doesn't love me, Luca. What do I have to do to make him love me?

The sweat turned to a chill. 'Does there have to be a reason? Maybe I was just born with good instincts for staying out of trouble.'

'You've spent your whole life in trouble.'

'I would argue I've spent my life having fun and pleasing myself.'

There was a tense silence and when she turned to him the warmth was gone from her eyes. 'You never let your guard down, do you? You insist that I don't hide anything from you but when it comes to your own secrets you're as impenetrable as Fort Knox. I thought what we had here was more than just superficial, but clearly that was my mistake.' Her voice was tart. 'No worries. Forget I ever asked. I'm not used to trusting people anyway so I have no idea why I'd start with someone like you.'

'Taylor—'

'No, really, you've made it clear you don't want to talk and that's fine with me.' It was obvious from her tone that it wasn't fine. She was all business. 'I gather Santo and Ella have agreed to let you use the set for the photo shoot this morning. I'm not a model but if you tell me what you want I'll do it.' No self-doubt. No insecurity. She didn't hunt for compliments or press him for reassurance that she'd be able to do the job.

It occurred to him that not once in all the time they'd spent together had she asked for reassurance about her appearance. In fact, she hadn't asked anything of him except to be her fake fiancé.

He tightened his grip on the steering wheel. 'I just want you to be yourself. Taylor Carmichael.'

'Which version?' She was back to being her usual guarded self and although he knew he should have been relieved, he missed the laughing version of the night before.

'The real version. You're edgy, modern, strong. Sure of who you are. It shows in the way you carry yourself, in the way you deal with people and in the way you face the world.

You're a self-sufficient high-achiever who has learned to depend on no one but yourself because everyone you've ever met has used you so you're not going to let that happen again.' He kept his eyes on the road as he described how he saw her. 'You were let down by your mother, by your father and by a man you trusted and every secret you ever had was blown over the pages of newspapers. It's left you vulnerable, but it's also given you strength because there's no way you're ever going to let anything like that happen to you again. You're so afraid of being hurt again you shut the world out and hide behind the tough-girl act. That's what I want to see when you're wearing the clothes.'

She was staring at him, her face pale. 'I—I've told you so much. Too much.' Her voice was a whisper. 'Why did I do that?'

'I don't know.' He was asking himself a similar question. 'Because you trusted me.'

'I don't trust anyone.' Her lips were bloodless and it took no effort to read her mind.

'You're worried I'll sell your story to the media?' He was surprised by how much that hurt. 'Come on, Taylor—'

'You've remembered every detail. Every single detail I've ever told you.'

'Because I'm a good listener.'

'Why? So that you don't forget the juicy parts?'

'You know me better than that.'

'I don't know you at all. You haven't let me know you.' She was stammering in her panic. 'I have no idea what you're capable of when you're upset or annoyed and I've trusted you with information I would never have given to anyone else.' She pressed shaking fingers to her face and breathed deeply while Luca swore under his breath and tried to grab hold of a situation that was fast spinning out of control.

But they'd arrived at the docklands and already the usual crowd of journalists pressed around the car.

Luca yanked on the handbrake. 'We need to talk.'

'I've talked.' There was no missing her emphasis on the word. 'The problem is you haven't and I'm not interested in a one-sided relationship.' Before he could respond Taylor was out of the car, tall, long-limbed and beautiful as she walked gracefully to where the modelling shoot was to take place.

He wanted to remind her their relationship was fake. That confidences had no part in what they were doing here. But the whole thing was a confused mess in his head and there was no opportunity to sort it out because the photo shoot was already under way.

And she was as professional during the shoot as she was with her acting. She listened to what was required and worked her heart out and by lunchtime Luca knew that what he had was perfect. Even the exacting, hypercritical Gianni was happy.

He had no idea how Taylor felt because the mask was back up and he knew it was his fault. Not only had he stripped away her protective shell and frightened her, he'd shut her down when she'd asked him a personal question.

I don't know you at all. You haven't let me know you.

Her words stayed with him as he walked into the boardroom an hour later. Prepared for something close to adulation from them for the way his ideas were already increasing occupancy and profits, Luca opened the door and was greeted by stony silence. A few of the older members of the board avoided looking at him.

Deciding that this was a day that definitely wasn't going his way, Luca strolled to the head of the table and braced himself for trouble. 'Well, this isn't quite the fun afternoon I was anticipating.' He kept his tone light but he was surveying the room, trying to identify the reason for the frosty atmosphere. 'Something wrong?'

There was an awkward silence.

The chairman cleared his throat. 'You don't know?'

'Know what?'

'About your fiancée.' The older man's mouth was set in a thin, disapproving line. 'It seems her past was even wilder than the rumours suggested. An Italian magazine claims to be in possession of certain naked photographs.'

Everything fell into place. He had no need to ask who had taken the photographs. Had no need to ask for any detail because he could guess at the detail all too easily.

Luca kept his face impassive. 'Photographs?'

'So you don't know.' The chairman exchanged a relieved glance with the rest of the board. 'Naturally this won't reflect well on you or the company. I expect you'll want to distance yourself from her actions and break off the engagement. It's damaging for the Corretti name and even more damaging for you personally.'

Closeted on the film set, it wasn't until Taylor finished filming for the day that she saw the usual crowd of journalists gathered at the barrier had swollen to ridiculous proportions.

Remembering the studio's insistence on publicity and determined not to give them any reason to complain about her, she forced herself to walk across to them. Her intention was to allow them a few shots that would hopefully satisfy them enough to make them leave her alone, but as she approached she sensed the buzz of excitement that comes with a major story.

'Taylor, do you have any comment on the photographs that are going to be published tomorrow?'

'Photographs?' But she knew what photographs and it was like stepping off a cliff.

The cameras were clicking away, microphones ready to record her response, and all she could do was stand there, staring at them in silence as the reality sank into her brain.

He'd done it.

Rafaele had finally done what he'd been threatening to do

for years. He'd sold the photographs. Photographs he'd had taken when she'd still thought there were people in the world who could be trusted. Photographs she hadn't even known existed until she'd broken up with him.

She'd often wondered how this moment would feel if it ever came but it felt nothing like she'd imagined.

She felt numb. Disconnected. As if she were watching events from the outside.

She'd expected to feel betrayed but she realised now the betrayal had come years before. And it had formed her. Influenced every choice she'd made since then. Tainted every affair and ruined every friendship.

'Taylor? The photographs are going to be published in an Italian magazine tomorrow.'

So not even somewhere far away. On Luca's home ground where it would cause him maximum humiliation. Soil his perfect shiny moment when his achievements were being lauded by the board.

Everyone was talking and the noise in her head grew and grew until she wanted to cover her ears and scream.

'I don't have any comment to make but I'll be contacting my lawyers.' But it wasn't her lawyers who she was thinking of as she forged her way to the black chauffeur-driven car that was always at her disposal during filming. It was Luca.

Luca, who was going to walk into that boardroom thinking that for once he had the upper hand only to be knocked unconscious by the weight of the secrets tumbling out of his fiancée's closet.

She knew he wouldn't care about the photographs—when had he ever cared what people thought—but he at least deserved some warning so that he was prepared to handle it.

Grateful for the blacked-out windows that gave her privacy, she leaned forward and ordered the driver to take her to the Corretti building as fast as possible.

The place was already swarming with press but with the

help of the security team employed by the studio, Taylor made her way through the glass doors unmolested.

Once inside, she took the elevator to the top floor and was about to ask where the board meeting was taking place when she saw Luca emerge from a room as if he were sleepwalking. His shirt was undone at the collar and he looked as if he'd been hit by a passing car. His handsome face was pale and his usually smooth hair tousled.

Eyes glassy, he knocked into a passing PA, sent a pile of papers flying and didn't even seem to notice. He didn't send her his trademark slanting smile, didn't use the opportunity to appraise her bare legs or make any comment at all.

It was clear that he was in shock and the fact that he was shocked shook her to the core.

Nothing shocked Luca.

Nothing.

Her insides lurched.

Slowly, he focused on her. His handsome face turned a shade paler and he didn't seem quite steady on his feet and for a moment he didn't speak. Just stared at her in disbelief as if he couldn't believe what he was seeing.

That shaken glance sent a tide of humiliation flowing over her and she realised just how much she'd been hoping he'd simply laugh at the whole thing. How much she'd been hoping they'd laugh together.

This was Luca Corretti. Bad boy personified. He was the one person she'd felt understood her. She'd wanted him to wink and say something in that careless voice of his—something like 'I hope they got your good side, *dolcezza*.'

Never, in all the time they'd been together, had she seen Luca Corretti at a loss for words. He always had a smart comeback for everything. He was never bothered by anyone's opinion.

But he was bothered now.

In fact, he looked as if he needed to lie down.

As if to confirm that, he turned to his PA. 'Get me a whisky.' His usual smooth, sexy voice was rough and shaky and when his stunned PA handed him a glass he drank it in one gulp, his hand trembling so badly he could barely hold the glass.

Then he looked at Taylor. 'I just found out— I had no idea— I learned something—' He was uncharacteristically inarticulate and Taylor suddenly found she had a lump lodged in her throat.

'I know you did.' She snapped the words, horrified to hear her own voice crack. 'I came to tell you myself. I'm sorry I was too late.'

'What did you come to tell me?' He looked distracted and she stared at him in exasperation.

'Well, obviously that— Oh, never mind—you already know. You found it out yourself.'

'Yes. Yes, I did and—*Cristo*, Taylor…'

The sight of him so shaken up unsettled her more than she wanted to admit. He'd seemed to understand her so well. Better than anyone ever had before. Why wasn't it obvious to him that Rafaele had taken advantage of her? He knew about her controlling mother and the way her father had used her. He knew she'd been vulnerable at the time. He knew all that and instead of defending her or even encouraging her to tell, he was shocked.

But of course he was.

Because he was thinking about himself, not her, the way people always did.

He'd agreed to the engagement as a means of gaining respectability and these revelations had just blown that out of the water. The board had probably just fired him, which would explain why he was reacting so strongly.

Taylor lifted her chin. 'I'm sorry you feel this way.'

'You are?' His voice was raw. 'You're sorry?'

'Of course! It wasn't what either of us wanted. It wasn't

part of our arrangement.' *I wanted your support.* Suddenly she was desperate to leave before she made a fool of herself.

'It's over, Luca. Done. Finished. The terms of our agreement have changed so that's the end of it. There's nothing more to be said.' She walked towards the door and then, because she just couldn't help herself, she made the mistake of looking back. And wished she hadn't because Luca was staring blindly into the distance, looking like a man who had lost everything.

CHAPTER NINE

TAYLOR LAY IN a sodden heap on her bed in her trailer where she'd spent the night, too drained to get up and face the press. She hadn't slept at all, just lain there, hoping desperately to hear from Luca. Hoping desperately that once he'd had time to think about it, he'd revert to his usual indifferent self and come and laugh with her.

But she heard nothing from him.

It seemed everyone in the world had called her except him. Everyone wanted her comment on the impending publication of the photographs, everyone wanted to know her side of the story and how she felt about the world seeing her naked. And she didn't even care. Each time her phone pinged with another message she grabbed it hopefully but it was never him. He didn't communicate. Not even a single text saying how sorry he was that she was in this mess.

She'd had no idea the pretence of respectability had mattered so much to him and the image of his shocked expression was jammed in her brain.

It wasn't just the thought of the whole world seeing her naked that upset her, it was the fact that Luca didn't care about how she felt. All he'd thought about was himself and how it was going to affect him. When she'd walked into his office yesterday she'd wanted him to defend her. Instead he'd looked shocked.

Luca Corretti, shocked.

He'd done shocking things in his life but clearly he was like so many men. He had double standards when it came to his own behaviour.

The weird thing was she didn't even care about the photographs any more. Even though it was what she'd dreaded for so long, she didn't care about the embarrassment and the humiliation. All she cared about was that her 'engagement' to Luca was over. No more dinners. No more skinny-dipping in the sea. No more Tomas and Teresa. No more…

Fat, scalding tears slid down her cheeks.

Reaching for another tissue, she blew her nose hard, acknowledging the truth with a sick lurch of her stomach.

She loved him.

Really loved him. All of him, from the fun outrageous side of him to the hurt, lonely boy who didn't trust anyone.

Somehow, somewhere, her feelings had shifted from fake to real whereas he—he didn't have any feelings at all.

There was a hammering on the door of her trailer but she covered her ears and screwed her eyes shut, ignoring it.

She'd faced the press alone so many times in her life, why did it feel harder this time?

But she knew the answer to that.

She'd allowed herself to trust Luca. For the first time since her teens, she'd lowered her guard. She'd believed he was a friend. But when trouble had landed he'd cut her loose and tried to distance himself.

She yanked another tissue out of the box. What had she expected? That he'd stand up and fight for her?

The hammering grew louder. It sounded as if they were actually going to kick the door down and anger flashed through her misery.

Why couldn't they leave her alone?

'Taylor! *Cristo*, open this door!' Luca's voice thundered through the door and Taylor jumped in shock.

'Go away! You are a hypocritical bastard and I never want to see you again.'

'Open the door or I'll break it down.'

'Fine! Whatever. If that's what you want.' Springing from the bed, she wrenched open the door and Luca immediately barged his way past her and slammed it shut, blocking out the cameras.

He swore in Italian. 'It's crazy out there.'

'Probably safer out there than in here.' Defensive anger bubbling up through the misery, Taylor folded her arms and tapped her foot on the floor but the words on her lips died as she took a proper look at him. 'You look awful. Isn't that the same suit you were wearing yesterday?'

'What? No. Yes.' He looked down at himself blankly and then back at her, tension in his features. 'I don't know. I do know there are things I need to say to you.'

'If "sorry for being a hypocrite" isn't on that list then you can save your breath and get out now.'

'Hypocrite?'

'Oh, come on, Luca—I saw your face yesterday. You were shocked.' The words choked her. 'How dare you be shocked? After everything you've done in your life.'

'But I've never done this.' His voice was hoarse. 'I just didn't think this would ever happen to me. I didn't want it to happen.'

'"This" being involved with someone like me? Well, I'm sorry to have disturbed your perfect life.' Tears of frustration and humiliation stung her eyes and she pointed to the door. 'Leave, before I sully your reputation even more. If you think you're such a saint, get out now. And it didn't happen to you, it happened to me. That's my naked butt up there on the Internet, not yours, so stop being so sanctimonious. You've done far worse, Luca Corretti. You are many things but I had no idea you were a hypocrite.'

He raked his hand over the back of his neck, his expression bemused. '*Cosa?* What are you talking about?'

'You! I just can't believe you're shocked to see naked photographs! You're the one who almost ripped my dress off at the wedding.' That revelation was met by tense silence.

'You think I'm shocked about the photographs?' Looking slightly dazed, he lowered his hand from the back of his neck. 'That's why you're calling me a hypocrite?'

'I saw you, Luca. Yesterday, when you stumbled out of the boardroom, you could barely speak you were so shocked.'

'Yes, but not about the photographs. I was shocked because—' he broke off and licked his lips '—because I...'

'Because what?'

He looked like a man who was about to step off a cliff. 'Because I'd just discovered I was in love with you. *Cristo*, that is the first time I've said it out loud and it sounds as weird as it feels.' He sank onto the edge of her bed and stared down at his hands. 'Look at me—I'm shaking.' He held out his hands as evidence but Taylor simply stared at him, stunned into silence by his raw confession.

Her mouth opened and shut but no sound came out and he looked at her helplessly.

'I've never been shocked by anything before but I was shocked by this. I still am. I'm a guy who has never fallen for a woman. I never intended to fall for a woman.' His voice was as shaky as his hands. 'When you started this engagement farce I thought I was going to hate every minute of it. Instead I loved every minute of it. I loved every minute of being with you. You're bright, sexy, funny, confident, sexy, strong, warm—did I say sexy?'

'Wait a minute.' It was Taylor's turn to shake. 'Are you really telling me you love me?'

'Yes and last night you said you were sorry I felt this way which, by the way, was not the most sympathetic comment I've ever heard.'

'Last night I thought you were shocked because there are going to be naked photographs of me everywhere. You're shocked because you love me?'

'Yes. And there won't be photographs. That's where I've been all night. With the Corretti family lawyers. We've stopped the photos being published.'

It was her turn to be shocked. 'How can you do that? The Italian press are notorious for not caring about rules and regulations.'

'There are some advantages to being a Corretti. We stopped it. That's all you need to know. No one gets to see my wife naked but me.'

'W-wife?'

'You have to marry me.' He was on his feet, his expression strained. 'Until I met you I'd never spent a whole night with a woman and now I can't stand being parted from you even for a moment. Even when I'm not with you I'm thinking about you all the time. I know you find it hard to trust people and I understand why, but I wanted to prove to you that you could trust me. I made sure those photographs won't be used.'

'But our engagement was fake. We did it because it gave us both respectability.'

He gave a humourless laugh. 'And how did that work for you, *dolcezza*? Because I hated every minute of being respectable. I don't care what anyone writes about you. I never have and never will.'

The fact he hadn't sold her out to the press meant almost as much as hearing him say he loved her. 'He told me I was beautiful. Rafaele...' The tears were falling again and she brushed them away with her palm. 'I was homeless and I had no one—my own mother had turned her back on me and my father had sold his story to the press, and he was there for me. Except that he wasn't. I trusted him—'

'Shh...' Luca wrapped her in his arms. 'He doesn't deserve a moment of your time and he certainly isn't worth your tears. Don't cry.'

'He's held it over me for so long. He didn't even tell me he had the photographs until after our relationship ended. He paid someone to take them from the garden of the house we were using in California. I had no idea. I thought it was just the two of us. I thought we were alone.' She pressed her face against his shirt and felt safe. 'And then I ended it and he told me what he had. How he'd use them. No matter where I went or what I did, he found me. And I always knew he was just waiting for the right time.' She swallowed, relieved to finally be able to tell someone. 'And the pressure got to me. Do you know how it feels to wake up every day wondering if this is the day the world is going to see you naked? It's just horrible. And finally—well, I had a sort of breakdown.'

'I know. I saw the pictures of you but no one knew what happened or where you went.'

'It wasn't drugs or drink. It was just the pressure. I wanted to get away. I flew out of LA and on the plane I met Zach.'

'Zach the friend?'

'That's all he ever was. He served in Iraq. We got talking and in the end I went back with him to DC and volunteered in a rehab unit. They didn't care who I was, they were just grateful for the help. I felt good about myself for the first time in my life. It was Zach who helped me separate the acting from all the mess that surrounds it.'

'I'm starting to almost like Zach.' Luca stroked her hair gently. 'So what made you come back to acting?'

'I read this script. And Zach helped me see that I love being an actress, I just hate being in the spotlight when I'm not on set. I hate that feeling that everyone is waiting to tear me down. And because of our engagement you'll be pulled down with me.' She felt sick when she thought of it. 'I dread to think what the board said to you.'

'They told me I had to distance myself from you and that's

when I realised I didn't want to. I didn't want it to be fake. I want it to be real.'

'Are you sure?' Her smile was wobbly. 'The real me gets me in trouble every time.'

'Never with me. You're forgetting that I grew up with fake. I grew up watching my mother turn herself inside out in an attempt to please my father.'

Taylor touched his face. 'You've never talked about her.'

'She worked so hard to make him love her.' His raw confession startled her and she eased away so she could look at him.

'You don't have to tell me this.'

'I want to. I want you to understand. But I'm not good at this—I've never talked to anyone.'

'Why do you say she was fake?'

'He hurt her again and again and she just came back for more and tried to be who she thought he wanted her to be. He travelled a lot and I used to dread him coming home. She went from being a relatively stable normal parent to an insecure mess. She'd walk into my room at all hours, sometimes she'd even wake me up, and she'd always be dressed in something different, wanting to know how she looked. "You have your grandfather's sense of style, Luca, tell me if this works. Will he like me in this?"' His handsome face revealed the strain. 'For a while, when I was very young, I actually thought that to be loved you had to wear the right clothes. And every time my father rejected her she'd study his latest girlfriend and try and copy the look and she'd ask me again, "Is this better? Do you think he'll like this?" And when he didn't I always blamed myself. Maybe if I'd told her to wear pink instead of cream. Or wear her hair up instead of down. Maybe if I'd got it right, she wouldn't have spent the whole night crying.'

Appalled, Taylor slid her fingers into his.

He'd shouldered responsibility for his parents' marriage. He'd taken on his mother's pain.

'No wonder you didn't want commitment.'

'To me, commitment meant being responsible for someone's feelings. It meant tying yourself in knots to be what
someone else wanted you to be. It was about losing your
sense of self. I had to watch her suffer every single day of
my life growing up.' His voice was raw. 'I saw that love
was manipulative and painful. I decided early on I didn't
want that.'

'No. I can see why you wouldn't.' Taylor hesitated and then
put her hand on his cheek. 'I'm no expert, but if love exists I
don't think that was it.'

'I know it wasn't.' He leaned his forehead against hers and
she gave an unsteady laugh.

'What a pair we are. We did this to give us both respectability. Thanks to me, your respectability has been blown
apart. I don't think it quite worked out the way either of us
planned.'

'I'm bored with being respectable. It makes me irritable. I want to be who I really am and I want to be it with
you.' Sliding his hand around her back, he pulled her hard
against him. 'How do you feel about doing this for real?'
He breathed the words against her lips. 'We can spend the
rest of our lives being disreputable together. We can live
wickedly ever after.'

It sounded so impossibly good that tears filled her eyes
and she blinked them away. 'Is that really what you want?'

'Yes. I love you, Taylor Carmichael Corretti. I love you
for better and for worse—preferably worse, by the way.' His
eyes glittered into hers. 'I love a bad girl. Think about it—if I
marry you we can spend the rest of our lives shocking people.'

She kissed him, half laughing, half crying and loving him
more than she'd thought it was possible to love a person.
'We'll be tomorrow's headlines.'

'You're with me now. You don't care if you're tomorrow's

headlines. Come on, Teresa, let's go and break a few rules together, with or without clothes. Your choice.'

She was smiling but the feeling of warmth grew and spread through her veins. 'Do you mean it? What you just said?'

'About it being real? About wanting to marry you? Definitely.'

'No one has ever loved me before. No one. You're not just worried about losing the new face of Corretti?'

'This isn't just the face of Corretti—' he stroked her cheeks with his thumbs, his eyes warm as he looked at her '—it's the face I want to see every night when I go to sleep and the face I want to see every morning when I wake up.'

The lump grew in her throat. 'I never knew you were so poetic.'

'Neither did I. I'm shocking myself.' He grinned and kissed her on the mouth until she pulled away.

'I love you too, but I'm worried I'll destroy your reputation. What about the board—'

'The board can sort themselves out. I've proved I can do it. I've increased their profits. Besides, hotels are boring.' He stifled a yawn. 'It's time my brother Matteo came back and got on with the job he's paid to do. All this respectability is making me uncomfortable. The other day they used the word *sobriety* in the same breath as my name. Can you believe that?'

Taylor gave a choked laugh. 'But what will you do? You're so brilliant and talented—will you focus on the fashion business?'

'I'll do what I do best which is living life to the full. Want to live it with me, *dolcezza*?'

She didn't need to think about it. Not even for a second. 'Yes,' she said simply, 'yes, I do.'

'*Bene*. In that case I take you, Taylor Carmichael, to have and to hold, to sin and misbehave with until too much hot sex doth leave us breathless and knackered. How does that sound to you?'

Laughing, unbelievably happy, she wrapped her arms round his neck. 'It sounds just perfect.'

* * * * *

*Read on for an exclusive interview
with Sarah Morgan!*

BEHIND THE SCENES
OF SICILY'S CORRETTI DYNASTY:

It's such a huge world to create—an entire Sicilian dynasty. Did you discuss parts of it with the other writers?

Whenever you take part in a series like this it's important to be consistent and link the books so, yes, there was discussion between the writers. We emailed back and forth discussing various aspects of the setting and characters and how we might bring it to life.

How does being part of the continuity differ from when you are writing your own stories?

When I write my own stories I create everything, including the setting, the characters, the backstory and the conflict. I don't have to think—or worry—about anyone else. In a continuity, the authors are given a large volume of background information to work with and that can be very challenging. Although there is some flexibility and freedom within the brief, I have to remember that any changes I make might impact on someone else's story. But I'm still writing a love story between two people and the focus is on their emotional journey so the basic process is the same.

What was the biggest challenge? And what did you most enjoy about it?

The biggest challenge is always being given an outline for two characters and the main plot points. Fortunately, I fell in love with these characters. From the moment I read the brief they came alive for me and I could "see" who they were and how their conflict would play out in the story.

As you wrote your hero and heroine, was there anything about them that surprised you?

I was surprised by just how bad Luca was. But I wasn't alone in that. Taylor was surprised, too. So we spent the book being surprised together!

What was your favorite part of creating the world of Sicily's most famous dynasty?

It was lovely to spend my day dreaming of Sicilian blue skies and the sparkling ocean, but the best part for me was writing the dialogue between the hero and heroine. I call this my "banter book." Taylor and Luca had so much fun together, even during the most emotionally charged intense moments of the story, and I had so much fun writing it.

If you could have given your heroine one piece of advice before the opening pages of the book, what would it be?

Beware of wickedly hot men bearing champagne.

What was your hero's biggest secret?

I never reveal a person's secrets! I can tell you that Luca is not a man who feels the need to hide who he is from anyone, but there are things he prefers not to talk about.

What does your hero love most about the heroine?

Apart from her legs? That she's every bit as bad as he is.

What does your heroine love most about your hero?

That he doesn't care what other people think of him.

Which of the Correttis would you most like to meet and why?

Luca! He's one of the most wickedly gorgeous heroes I've written and I love his sense of humor. I know a night with him would be something no woman would forget!

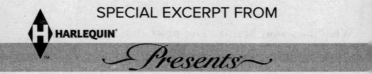
* * *

"I will not leave you again." It was a vow, accompanied by the slipping of the ring onto her finger.

Even though it was prompted by her pregnancy and the fact she now carried the heir to the Volyarus throne, the promise in his voice poured over the jagged edges of her heart with soothing warmth. The small weight of the metal band and diamonds on her finger was a source of more comfort than she would ever have believed possible.

She was not sure her heart would ever be whole again, but it did not have to hurt like it had for ten weeks.

"I won't leave you, either."

"I know." A small sound, almost a sigh, escaped his mouth. "Now we must convince your body that it still belongs to me."

"You have a very possessive side."

"This is nothing new."

"Actually, it kind of is." He'd shown indications of a possessive nature when they were dating, but he'd never been so primal about it before. "You're like a caveman."

His smile was predatory, his eyes burning with sensual intent. "You carry my child. It makes me feel *very* possessive, takes me back to the responses of my ancestors."

Air escaped her lungs in an unexpected whoosh. "Oh."

"I have read that some pregnant women desire sex more often than usual."

"I…" She wasn't sure what she felt in that department right now.

She always seemed to want him and could not imagine her hormones increasing that all too visceral need.

"However, I had not realized the pregnancy could impact the father in the same way." There was no mistaking his meaning.

Maks wanted her. And not in some casual, sex-as-physical-exercise way. The expression in his dark eyes said he wanted to devour her, the mother of his child, sexually.

Gillian shivered in response to that look.

"Cold?" he purred, pushing even closer. "Let me warm you."

"I'm not co—" But she wasn't allowed to finish the thought.

His mouth covered hers in a kiss that demanded full submission and reciprocation.

* * *

Find out what happens when this powerful prince raises the stakes of their marriage of convenience in ONE NIGHT HEIR, out July 2013!

And don't miss the explosive second story, PRINCE OF SECRETS, available August 2013.

REQUEST YOUR FREE BOOKS!

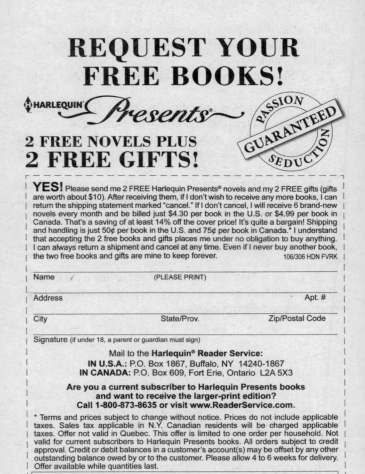

HARLEQUIN *Presents*

PASSION GUARANTEED SEDUCTION

2 FREE NOVELS PLUS
2 FREE GIFTS!

YES! Please send me 2 FREE Harlequin Presents® novels and my 2 FREE gifts (gifts are worth about $10). After receiving them, if I don't wish to receive any more books, I can return the shipping statement marked "cancel." If I don't cancel, I will receive 6 brand-new novels every month and be billed just $4.30 per book in the U.S. or $4.99 per book in Canada. That's a saving of at least 14% off the cover price! It's quite a bargain! Shipping and handling is just 50¢ per book in the U.S. and 75¢ per book in Canada.* I understand that accepting the 2 free books and gifts places me under no obligation to buy anything. I can always return a shipment and cancel at any time. Even if I never buy another book, the two free books and gifts are mine to keep forever.   106/306 HDN FVRK

Name _____ (PLEASE PRINT) _____

Address _____ Apt. # _____

City _____ State/Prov. _____ Zip/Postal Code _____

Signature (if under 18, a parent or guardian must sign)

Mail to the **Harlequin® Reader Service:**
IN U.S.A.: P.O. Box 1867, Buffalo, NY 14240-1867
IN CANADA: P.O. Box 609, Fort Erie, Ontario L2A 5X3

**Are you a current subscriber to Harlequin Presents books
and want to receive the larger-print edition?
Call 1-800-873-8635 or visit www.ReaderService.com.**